Idyll with Drowning Dog

and

Madalyn

Studies in Austrian Literature, Culture, and Thought

Translation Series

Michael Köhlmeier

Idyll with Drowning Dog

Translated by
David Dollenmayer

Ariadne Press
Riverside, California

Ariadne Press would like to express its appreciation to the Worcester Polytechnic Institute for its assistance in publishing this book.

Library of Congress Cataloging-in-Publication Data

Köhlmeier, Michael, 1949-
Dollenmayer, David B., translator
　Köhlmeier, Michael, 1949- Idylle mit ertrinkenden Hund. English
　Köhlmeier, Michael, 1949- Madalyn. English
　Idyll with drowning dog and Madalyn/Michael Köhlmeier; translated by David Dollenmayer
　　(Studies in Austrian literature, culture, and thought. Translation series)
　　ISBN 9781572412002 (pbk.)
Köhlmeier, Michael, 1949---Translations into English/Fathers and daughters---Fiction/Novellas.
　PT2671.O344 A2 2016
　833/.914—dc23　　　　　　　　2016000288

Cover Design: George McGinnis
Copyright 2016
by Ariadne Press
270 Goins Court
Riverside CA 92507
Translation © 2010 by David Dollenmayer

All right reserved.
No part of this publication may be reproduced or transmitted in any form or by any means without formal permission.
Printed in the United States of America.
ISBN 9781572412002
Paperback original.

Translator's Dedication

In Memoriam

Asher Green
1979-2007

Author's Dedication

For Monika,
Oliver,
Undine,
Lorenz,
and for our dear Paula.

The two of them sit by the Old Rhine waiting for the angel, hoping perhaps he'll spend the night with them. It's cold, but they don't dare sleep in the car for fear of missing the angel. Surely the angel won't wait for us, they think. If we're sleeping, the angel won't wake us up.

Paula Köhlmeier
The Two of Them

1

Dr. Beer edited only three of my books. He broke off work on the fourth "in view of the state of my health," as he informed me in a handwritten letter. I know better. He felt ashamed in my presence because of what happened during our last project together: the incident with the dog. It may be that he wouldn't approve of my telling the story here. He was more than just my editor, however. He was my teacher too, and always insisted that a literary work is worthless if it makes concessions to anything or anyone.

Only a few days before the incident in question, he had begun addressing me with the familiar *du*. It was the last thing I would have expected! I couldn't even imagine him saying *du* to his own wife (of whose existence—and after all, we had known each other for eight years!—I had no knowledge at the time). I never associated the man with concepts such as "wife," "girlfriend," "lover," or anything having to do with a family. Not even parents figured in my mental image of him; similarly, categories of the ages of man such as "childhood" or "youth" resisted being used to describe his life as in any way comparable to, say, mine. The very thought of henceforth calling him "Johannes" made me uptight and promised to do so forever. Naturally, I avoided it. It was obvious—almost insultingly obvious—that he couldn't get used to calling me by my first name either.

Only once did I ever say his first name: when I introduced him to my wife. "*Das ist der Johannes*," I said. In our Alemanic vernacular, we put the definite article in front of someone's name, which must have sounded crude to him. That was OK with me; the article *der* clearly increased the distance between his skin and mine, re-

2

established an order I was satisfied with because it was as reliable as the temperature at the bottom of the sea.

Nevertheless, I admit it would have pleased me to just once hear *my* first name from *his* lips—as an act of reciprocity, an equals sign between his weight and mine. I was never able to rid myself of the feeling that he was testing me in small, covert ways, not necessarily to catch me out in an error but just to keep tabs on me in a sort of consensual paternalism—quite benevolently (which would make it even worse). No sooner had I spoken his name than I was ashamed I'd done it. He noticed. It was as if I had beaten him to it and discovered his weak point before he'd gotten his sights on mine. He turned to Monika and called her—was he trying to prove something?—"Frau Köhlmeier."

He'd let drop that initial *du* on the telephone—by accident, as I soon became convinced. Perhaps when I called him up there had been someone in the room he was on intimate terms with and my call had burst in on their conversation—I couldn't imagine that was the case, however, for the simple reason that I couldn't imagine him having any close friends, and I was certain he would have allowed only such to call him *du*. What seemed more likely was that he had just been reading a book or manuscript with a particularly good passage in which—who knows?—maybe two friends were talking, and he was so immersed in that invented world that for a few seconds after he picked up the phone, he was unable to shake off the fictive world's sound and carried it with him, in thought, into the receiver and from there right into my ear.

But even that explanation didn't seem plausible. Dr. Beer was my editor. He was sixty by that time and esteemed as one of the most competent by anyone who knew anything about German publishing. Up to that point, aside from the weather and the traffic in Frankfurt, he and I had never talked about anything except literature and I don't know of anyone who figured out how to sustain a conversation with him on any other topic. And yet, I'd always suspected him of not really being interested in novels and stories, novellas and essays—plots, characters, dialogues; of being simply *not* interested in literature, but only in its virtuoso manipulation. Something quite different was dear to his heart, I thought. Mind you, I didn't have the slightest idea what that thing might be. A man leading a double life? He would have drawn a wavy line under that phrase in my manuscript and when we were working together and got to the passage would have said, "Personally, you know, I like such words and I just wish you had used them in a more appropriate context, but here I must ask you to replace them with something else."

"I'm Lear's fool," he once said of himself. Which left open the question of who his Lear was. After all, who would want to compare himself with that Man of Sorrows?

No one knew what he did after he put on his coat, turned up his collar, said goodbye to the receptionist at the entrance to the publisher's offices, opened his umbrella, and disappeared round the corner—not even if he went home by taxi or bus, by subway or in his own car, by bicycle or on foot. Home? What did his home look like? Floor-to-ceiling bookcases occupied the walls of his office and unlike the books of the senior editor for non-fiction (aside from a shelf of reference works, her books were all the products of that publisher), his books conveyed the impression that they were his private library. German classics were parked next to poets Russian and American, the collected works of D. H. Lawrence, Joseph Conrad (his favorite author and mine), and Luigi Pirandello, poetry from France and Ireland, but mainly works of philosophy. He had told me—curtly, brusquely, and only after I'd asked him twice—that he'd majored in philosophy and written his dissertation on an aspect of Husserl's phenomenology. Works by and about Husserl comprised a good quarter of his library. So, did his writing and reading life—his intellectual life—take place only there, in his office? Well why shouldn't they? And in his spare time did he go bowling with lawyers and tax accountants or belong to a biker club or go bar-hopping with his buddies? Well why not? Of course, I couldn't imagine that this man had any buddies, and that was because I didn't *want* to imagine that he had any private life at all.

Nobody knows anything about the private life of Lear's fool, either. And no one knows if he believes what he says. Words are the fool's tools; he knows no other.

And then on the telephone, after the pronoun *du* had slipped out in an unguarded moment, he said, "I suggest that in the future we address each other *in this way*."

The word itself could not be retracted either by him or by me without causing insult. And yet he had taken such pains not to say the word again in the way he had worded his suggestion . . .

What's more, he went on to propose that instead of me coming to Frankfurt to work on the manuscript, he should come to me in Hohenems – and was promptly shocked at himself (this was transparently clear to me), but by then there was no going back on that either. I guessed that he had failed to adequately assess the consequences of the new situation, i.e., that a *du* must be followed up with a bit of concrete action so that it's more than just an option hanging over every further word like a stalactite about to fall, and now he'd gotten himself into an even more uncomfortable situation.

While still holding the receiver in my hand, I looked out the window as if *in this way* I could avoid the impact of intimacy. A silence had begun between us and it was like a contest. I heard, he heard, how he, how I each tinkered with a sentence in which the tiny word could be housed, in his for the second time, in mine for the first, yet in both cases without embarrassment. I could picture him in my mind's eye (a slight man, not large, with quick, purposeful movements unique to him); he would shake his head slightly as he began his sentence and shake it again as he ended it.

It was snowing so hard that I could only make out the neighboring house in outline. It had been snowing for weeks. It was January, the snowy winter of 2006. I recalled Dr. Beer once telling me that he went for a walk every day for at least an hour and had been doing so since his thirtieth birthday.

I said, "When you come . . ."—*Wenn* du *kommst* (I was unable to not stress the word)—". . . bring along a pair of sturdy shoes for our walks and a warm hat and coat too."

"I will," he said. "Do you like this winter?"

"Do you?" I asked in return.

"Yes, very much," he said. "*Und du?*"

"I don't think I do, actually."

When my father died in the early eighties, Monika and I and the children had moved into my parents' house in Hohenems. The street was almost completely unchanged from my childhood. Our neighbor had stuccoed his house at some point, that was all. A little tin pipe still sticks out of his roof. I never did know what it was for, but for my sister and me it was the yardstick for snow. I can remember only one time, it must have been in the early sixties, when there was nothing left of it to see, nothing except a slight bump. Now, there wasn't even a bump. The pipe was entirely buried in the masses of snow on the roof. During the past week I'd gotten up in the dark every morning at seven to shovel free the walkway to our front door. The mailman had made it clear in no uncertain terms that he wouldn't deliver the mail otherwise. I confined my efforts to a narrow path (just barely wide enough for a sled) and to its right and left rose piles of snow taller than a man. What was annoying was that the snowplow didn't come by until after the mailman and blocked off our entrance again; sometimes it came down our street once more in the afternoon, and not infrequently a third time in the evening.

Monika and I hardly left the house at all. We took the sled and went shopping every third day at most. The path over the Schlossberg that Monika usually hikes six times a week no matter what the weather was utterly impassable. She had tried it and given up; by the time she rounded the first switchback she was already up to her chest in drifts. Through binoculars from our kitchen window we could see the forest above the rock face. The fir trees were featureless white cones and looked more like art works by Christo and Jeanne-Claude than the works of nature.

I asked if I should reserve a room for him.

"No," he said without hesitation or further comment.

"It's simple," was Monika's interpretation once I had hung up and recapitulated the conversation for her in all its details. "He wants to stay with us. It's very simple: he's your friend now and a friend doesn't make a friend stay in a hotel."

"My friend?"

"What else? About time, too. Is there anyone you've surrendered more of yourself to in the last few years?"

"What does 'surrendered myself' mean?"

"I don't need to define the word for you." (*He* would subject the word to a thorough examination.)

"I've surrendered more of myself to you, for instance."

"OK, but otherwise?"

"Of course," I argued weakly, "it's also possible he prefers to have his secretary reserve a room for him. He doesn't want to put me to any trouble. Maybe that's what he meant."

"Have her reserve a room from Frankfurt? Here in Hohenems? Is there even a hotel here except for the Gasthaus Schiffle, where the innkeeper almost broke your nose forty years ago?"

Nevertheless, it seemed even less likely that in the few minutes of our telephone conversation, that cultivated man, without the slightest warning, could have sidled up so close to my life, and that this had happened not at all by accident, but in fact on purpose. Or had there been some warning signals I missed?

What does *surrender myself* mean?

"Be careful with that phrase!" he would say. "Don't use it unless you're conscious of its dichotomy, namely, the commingling of pain and pleasure. The person who surrenders himself is afraid to do so but also wishes to be hurt at the same time. If this seems like too great a load of significance for your purposes, then don't use that phrase. Replace it with something weaker: describe a piece of clothing instead, a gesture, or a facial expression (but be careful not to overdramatize faces!), or stick in a precise observation, a little parenthetical essay, or a memory, *en passant* as it were, but don't forget to take it up at greater length later so it isn't left teetering on one leg and feeling like a random insertion."

Analyzing a text with him was an adventure that could lead deep into unknown, incalculable darkness and be extremely time-consuming. Colleagues who published with other houses envied me working with him. For them, meeting with their editor about a novel of two hundred pages took one day maximum. In most cases, editors mailed back the corrected manuscript, authors entered the corrections into their text at the computer (provided they accepted them), and disagreements were discussed on the phone. End of story. At this Dr. Beer could only shake his head (economically, as was his wont). His model was Maxwell Perkins who edited Ernest Hemingway, F. Scott Fitzgerald, and Thomas Wolfe. Legend has it that from a stack of more than fifteen hundred manuscript pages, it took Perkins a year of work to construct the mere seven-hundred-page novel we know as *Look Homeward, Angel*. Dr. Beer also liked to talk about Gordon Lish, Raymond Carver's editor. He showed me the last manuscript page of one of Carver's stories and beside it the published version edited by Lish, which was first of all only a quarter the length and secondly didn't contain a single word of the original, i.e., it had been not just re- but completely newly written by Lish and, Dr. Beer assured me, without obtaining Carver's permission to do so. As a matter of fact, Dr. Beer regarded such a conception of the role of an editor as criminal, but he smiled when he said so—an ironic smile, protective or conspiratorial depending on whether you interpreted it as addressed to Carver or to Lish. (My money was on conspiratorial, that is, he felt himself an accomplice of Gordon Lish's, who often boasted to critics that he was Raymond Carver's ventriloquist and that the radically elliptical style we know as Carver's was the result of his editing and thus his invention—the critics, however, didn't believe him because Lish's own books were all flops.)

On the occasion of Dr. Beer's sixtieth birthday, the Saturday supplement of the *Frankfurter Allgemeine Zeitung* carried a long interview with him (title: "Mister Precision") in which he described how he worked. Very early in his career, he explained, he had made the following discovery: if it doesn't sound good to your ear, there's something inherently wrong with it. That's why he insisted that authors read questionable passages aloud to him—once, twice, three times.

That, dear Monika, is surrender!

When I listened to my own voice during this procedure, it was nothing but a device for detecting my own inadequacies and I got to feeling afraid of that mysterious (a word he really hated) person who was me, who went under my name, and obviously possessed more right to exist than I did myself, I who was simply fulfilling my role as Dr. Johannes Beer's assistant. He laid over certain passages a surgeon's drape with a slit in the middle to isolate the object of attention from all other organs, the better to investigate the meaning and resultant emanation of a single word within the clause and beyond that, within the sentence, as if he thought it possible that we were conversing in two different languages that only happened to sound the same. It was my text he trusted, not me the author. I trusted my editor but lost trust in my text. I was always prepared to discover in the blink of an eye that what I had thought was a consonance would turn out to be a mistake, since after all, mutual understanding has no other basis than "the words, the words, the words . . ." And yet it was I who was always demanding *Make me better*!

And was *he* at last rising up to demand something in return? Namely, an equals sign between his weight and mine? Was he insisting on his right to surrender to *me*? On long walks through the snow, for instance, which would end—provided no other rational beings were in sight—with us embracing, each clasping the back of the other's neck robustly enough so it doesn't seem like a caress: two men of advanced age and more or less fixed principles, two friends?

"That's probably it, exactly," said Monika. "It makes perfect sense to me. You represent all the authors he's ever edited. You just happen to be the last one. His last author, his last book."

"You really think so?" I asked.

"I think it's good for *you* to think so. And maybe that's really the way it is."

The next afternoon I picked him up at the station. He heaved his suitcase onto the sled—a big aluminum suitcase so heavy it suggested he was intending to stay three weeks with us—and together we pulled the sled across the street that was still a trail covered with more tracks of skis and sled runners than car tires.

"If it starts snowing again, it'll be hard to go for walks," I said.

10

Monika was waiting for us in front of the house. She'd thrown my old moss-green lumberjack shirt with the leather trim over her shoulders and was waving to us. It had gotten noticeably warmer since morning. The sky had been blue all day, like April. Now clouds were gathering again, but not snow clouds. I was hoping for a foehn, the warm dry wind that blows down the north slope of the Alps. But it would have its work cut out for it to put an end to this spectacle.

Dr. Beer tapped me on the arm (which gave me déjà-vu, as if someone in another life had warned me of an impending disaster in just this way). In a quiet voice that Monika couldn't hear, he said, "Listen, please don't be offended, but every day I need to go for a walk for at least two hours *alone*. It *has* to be alone. No matter what. I need a *walk*, and it has to be *by myself*."

Then he touched me again, this time patting my waist, left the sled rope to me, and hurried forward toward Monika with his arm extended. He greeted her so cordially that she looked at me with her brow furrowed in inquiry, since I had warned her that this Dr. Beer never smiled.

I could hear from her voice that she liked him immediately. And he liked her too.

2

He liked her even more when we brought him into the house and on into the living room. Once he'd shed his coat and exchanged his sturdy winter boots for a pair of brown suede slippers (fished from his suitcase surreptitiously and quick as a flash), I showed him Monika's jungle that runs riot along the windows on the opposite side of the room in a built-out extension with a greenhouse ceiling, a good twenty feet long and six feet deep; an ingeniously beguiling profusion of ferns, hart's-tongue, African hemp, aspidistra, a gigantic rubber plant, a philodendron, a miniature dragon tree, a grove of bonsais covering the platform formerly occupied by our Christmas crèche and suspended from the ceiling on four ivy-entwined chains, papyrus, flamingo flowers, anthurium, amaryllis, hibiscus, azaleas, passion flowers, something like fifty cacti from button to bowling ball size, ranged one above the other on delicate metal shelves, and many other plants whose names Monika never tires of drumming into me even though I always forget them again. In among them are totem poles of wood, plastic, and soldered together Coke cans, two slim, severe marble figures by a sculptor friend of ours, lavishly framed images of various sizes, clipped from newspapers and none of them having anything to do with wilderness or forests, Chinese pinwheels of tin, a Boeing 747 that's made an emergency landing on the slanting trunk of a lemon tree, a chameleon that changes color when you touch it, a dozen little monkeys, King Kong and Tyrannosaurus rex, a leopard and a panther, both porcelain and life-size, lizards, dragonflies, butterflies, hundreds of birds; then, the thing that perhaps catches a visitor's eye first: the dolls with their everlasting Mona Lisa smiles, the masks with irisless eyes, lost in thought and staring into the room; and across all of it teem tropical flowers made of silk and a huge variety of other materials produced by the plastics industry, so that one could believe that waiting here (or lying in wait) is a foreign, humid world in the middle of which beats the heart of darkness—not off somewhere on the upper reaches of the Congo in the ivory kingdom of Mister Kurtz, to be sure, but in a single-family house that looks quite staid from the outside, here in the middle of the snowiest winter of all time.

In his rapture, Dr. Beer's voice slipped into falsetto. He put his hands up to his cheeks. Uttered cries. "Unimaginable!—*Ach!*—*Mein Gott!*—Unbelievable!" Twice, three times he ran back and forth in front of the flower pots, flower tables, flower stands, from the end of the sofa on the right to the terrace door on the left and back again, looking like a bustling secretary on her way to the copy machine, which caused me not just astonishment but an embarrassed uneasiness—and impatience, too, since I began to suspect I had misjudged the possibilities and options of this man. Monika's jungle reveals the character of the person looking at it— that's what a friend once said. For sixteen years this friend had run a clinic for addicts, so I believed his every word.

Was he allowed to touch the plants? Dr. Beer cried.

"You have to tell me which ones are artificial and which are real," Monika challenged him.

We often played this game with guests. It's not so easy to tell the artificial from the natural and Monika was prepared to hear all possible expressions of amazement. She'd never been disappointed by the responses. Dr. Beer slipped off his sport coat, pushed his sweater and shirt sleeves above his elbows, closed his eyes, and plunged both arms deep into the tangled mass of green, yellow, red, pink, white, turquoise, violet, and blue. Meanwhile he kept cooing and giving little high-pitched yelps.

Monika laughed out loud, tilted her head toward me, and said softly – but not so softly he couldn't hear every word – "He's a lot funnier than you described him."

I wanted to sink into the ground!

"That's interesting," he called out, his eyes still closed and his arms still buried in the jungle. "No one has ever called me funny before."

He was palpating branches and blossoms, his fingers shrank back from a real cactus, stroked the inside of a plastic orchid blossom, tested the beak and talons of a parrot, rubbed a stiff, glassy petal as if it were a coin, cautiously tapped the backs of praline-sized beetles made of disgustingly realistic plastic and climbing caravan-style up a fuzzy stem.

"In our house, funny means funny peculiar," Monika explained to him. "So a funny man can be someone who's never laughed once in his whole life. But he's got to be peculiar—if that makes you feel any better."

He withdrew his arms, which had a summer tan and were as smooth and sinewy as a young man's, opened his eyes, turned toward her and touched her hip briefly the same way he had patted my waist as we were coming down Johann-Strauss-Strasse with his suitcase.

"My God, what a pleasure," he sighed. "Are there other animals living in this jungle besides beetles and parrots?"

"Snakes and lizards," said Monika, reached behind the coffee tree (a real one; she had grown it from white coffee beans the SPAR grocery store had sold for home roasting as a gimmick about ten years ago; its capacious branches constituted the foundation of the jungle), and produced a green mamba of soft, rubbery plastic which she jiggled in his face. He screamed, screamed a second time and a third—the first time from real fright, the second to be polite, but the third time as if to say (my interpretation) 'I think you're as beautiful as the jungle you created.' Yes, I was convinced that's exactly what he was thinking. I would have bet my knowledge of human nature on it, without which I might as well close up shop, but of course, he would have denied it with the argument that although perhaps he was funny as in funny peculiar, he wasn't stupid, and it would be a sign of stupidity in a man to compare a woman to a jungle. Words, words, words—wherever one was to be found, it created a fact. He was as convinced of that as Hamlet was.

"My jungle is walkable, by the way," said Monika. Her voice now sounding serious and somewhat shy as well. "Sometimes I go into the jungle, plop down, and then just sit there doing nothing. Come on, I'll show you the way."

From the eastern end, you can duck under a branch of the coffee tree, push aside a curtain of vines (also real and rooted somewhere or other, probably in the pots that hang down from the beam that supports the greenhouse roof and that Monika has painted with voodoo masks), and then you can see a narrow path laid with raffia mats. It leads all the way through the forest over to the couch. At first, Monika only intended to install a pretty, medium-size winter garden under the slanted glass roof. Flower pots stood on tall wooden tables she'd bought at flea markets and varnished in their natural colors. Over the years, the winter garden had turned into a jungle and finally burst the bounds of interior decoration, so that not all the plants could still be watered and pruned from the periphery and she had to lay out this path. There were places where you could squat down or simply stand without moving and people in the living room couldn't see you, at least not at night when the forest was illuminated only by the two ceiling lights – and not in the daytime either if you were wearing camouflage clothing or a Hawaiian shirt.

Monika pushed the vines aside and Dr. Beer entered. As far as I could remember, he was the first person aside from the members of our family to whom Monika had granted this privilege. (She hadn't even shown the path to our friend the former drug treatment clinic director, even though he was planning to shoot a documentary entitled "Monika's Jungle.") If he wanted, she'd be happy to supply him with a flashlight, she called after him, so he could see the details better—she called loudly on purpose, her hands cupped megaphone-style to her mouth as though he was already lost. (Sometimes she gets the urge to attend to the plants at night; then she takes a flashlight into the forest. I also suspect her of occasionally taking a pillow and blanket and stretching out on the path. She denies it, but always with a lovely broad grin.) The flashlight hangs from a hook beside the entrance. She handed it to him, then turned off the living room lights. The beam of the flashlight flitted through the forest, picking out leaves and blossoms and casting fleeting shadows.

What happened next threw me into such confusion that for a moment it felt like I was ejected from the scene. *Dr. Beer started singing and dancing.* It was a mere twenty minutes since he entered our house, twenty minutes since I'd racked my brain about how we were going to even carry on an everyday conversation with this man—and now *he was singing and dancing,* singing a tune he had invented on the spot to a text he had invented the same instant, a list of the things he was seeing with the words "I am" placed in front of each one:

"I am the monkey that laughs. I am the parrot with the bright comb. I am the spider with hairy legs. I am the crocodile hanging from a branch by his tail. I am the roaring plastic lion looking for someone to devour. I am the cruel, bloodthirsty stuffed tiger . . ."

Monika kept two conga drums she had given me for my fortieth birthday at the farthest end of the forest, near the sofa; a pair of bongos hung from a branch of the coffee tree. Dr. Beer set the flashlight in a flower pot; his face, illuminated from below, looked like an African mask commanding devotion and demanding sacrifices as he sang and danced and drummed.

When he emerged from the jungle and Monika turned the lights back on, he was embarrassed, as though we had caught him at some indecent act. All three of us were embarrassed. We stood there for a while like people who have strayed into a different time: the drummer from the forest (not at all one of us) and we, whom he had tried to seduce (not at all ourselves).

Finally, he took Monika's hand and held it while he said, "You open your heart to inspection. Forgive me for my behavior. But it wasn't all my fault."

Then he sank into one of the blood red easy chairs at the western end of the forest and clapped his hands. "Yes, it's a good bargain, really worth the trade-off. A third of this room as the price for enough fantasy to fill ten houses. Why haven't you ever offered me one of *your* novels?"

"Oh come on!" said Monika with a dismissive wave and to make sure the subject didn't come up again, she changed her expression. "We thought we'd go out to eat. There's an interesting restaurant where we've made a reservation. We just have to call a taxi." It seemed to me that her voice suddenly had a bitter undertone. "Personally, I don't care that much about fabulous meals, but people who do care leave this restaurant as if they'd discovered true religion."

He never took his eyes off her. "Interesting odd or interesting remarkable? Do they have a jungle like this one, for instance?"

"No."

"And do they have carpets under the tables like in an Arabian seraglio?"

"Not that I know of."

"And do they have red armchairs like these standing around?"

"Uh-uh."

"Then I don't want to go there."

I had noticed that he often uttered little absurdities as a prelude to weighty topics and I'd always interpreted this quirk as a way of cooling himself down. Of course, that assumed that precisely on weighty topics (namely, as he once explained to me, topics that succeeded in portraying the life of man as a "chameleonic thing," as Kleist called it), he was inclined to pathos and sentimentality and knew it. Such a topic was obviously at hand—the whole time he hadn't taken his eyes off her.

"Let's stay here as long as we can," he said. "If I come back in two years, I assume we'll have to clear ourselves a campsite with a Bowie knife."

I burst out laughing and immediately regretted it.

After Monika had completed her jungle in its present form, she sank into a deep depression; she blamed herself for ruining the basis of our life together, while I thought she was suffering from a creative urge that was like an addiction and I was seized by panic because I foresaw that from day to day, from week to week, the rank growth would make our living room impenetrable, transform our kitchen into an enchanted cavern on a Caribbean isle, that the walls, the ceilings, the pictures, the dolls, the stones picked up along the Schlossberg path, objects found at the flea market or discovered on the street—that all this would swallow us up and digest us, but at the same time I knew that without this ambience I would no longer feel good, if I was banned from this Altamira I couldn't go on living.

"Maybe you could make something for us?"

"I've forgotten how to cook," she said. "The only things I still know how to make are mashed potatoes and rice pudding."

"Rice pudding, then," he cried, his voice rising up out of the bass range as if he were already shoveling it in, "rice pudding it shall be! We must have rice pudding!!"

But there was melancholy in his eyes.

In the meantime, it had started to rain and the foehn had sprung up with a vengeance. Monika suggested we all walk along the Schillerallee beside the brook to the gas station. The sidewalk was shoveled and wide enough to walk three abreast. Attached to the gas station there's a minimart open twenty-four seven. The fact was, we had no milk in the house.

It was so warm we only wore jackets. I didn't even button mine up. Monika and I shared an umbrella, holding fast to the handle so it wouldn't blow inside out. Dr. Beer walked beside us, wearing a hat of kangaroo leather (he showed us the label to prove it) secured with a leather chin strap. He had conjured it from the depths of his suitcase.

At the gas station I showed him the beginning of the path that I walk five days a week alone and on Saturdays with Monika, the one I would loan him, starting tomorrow, for one or two or three walks, depending on how long the work on my manuscript took. The path goes past a home improvement store, crosses the bridge over the canal, and continues through the fields to the autobahn underpass; there you can decide if you want to go down to the water and along the Old Rhine or stay on the asphalt path that runs along beside the autobahn for a bit until the highway turns right and the path left. I prefer the higher path even though the lower one is certainly more beautiful and above all, quieter. Up on the asphalt I have open sky; down below I'm walking beneath the trees and it feels like a tunnel.

It was raining and blowing so hard that we could only converse by yelling. I was worried about the studio out in our garden. Its flat roof covers quite a large area and I guessed there must be five feet of snow on it. The rain would double its weight. Just a few days ago, the roof of a sports facility in Bad Reichenhall in Bavaria had collapsed under the weight of the snow. While Monika cooked the rice pudding, I was planning to shovel at least some of the snow from the roof.

Dr. Beer said if I wouldn't mind, he'd like to help.

The big stand of bamboo on the south side of our property was bent over by the masses of snow. I'd have to saw off most of the stalks come spring; in my experience they would not straighten up again. I had grown the cherry tree from a pit as a child and it had never needed a graft. Now its branches were drooping down into the garden. Soon after we moved into the house, Monika had planted ivy, Himalayan knotgrass, a rambler rose, and several other climbing vines around its base, which resulted in the tree blooming three or four times a year, but now it presented the snow with a lot of surface area and quite a few branches were broken. It looked like some natural disaster had hit. The branches of the Gravenstein apple tree next to the studio were resting against the edge of the roof. The foehn sent gusts into its crown, knocking down wide plops of snow. The seed balls we had tied to the branches for the titmice were all pecked almost clean, their nylon nets fluttering, breaking loose, and disappearing into the darkness. That winter, Monika and I had begun to bird-watch. We'd hung more bird feeders in the apple tree next to our kitchen window. During breakfast we watched bluetits and chickadees and sparrows and blackbirds and once, a pair of goldfinches. After only a few days of this, I was overcome by a sense of reverence and began to reflect upon life. It put me into a mood that reminded me of my youth and sprang either from my despair or from a cosmic optimism that was more fit for spring than winter. The starlings' house wore a tall cap of snow and had tipped forward. I couldn't imagine any living thing finding shelter in there.

Dr. Beer and I scrambled up a ladder onto the roof and stood in the storm like sappers, shovels in hand. When we looked over toward the house we could see the outlines of Monika's forest behind the wide picture window. Briefly, we saw her silhouette as she entered the living room. She put her hands up to her hair and lifted it away from her neck. I began to shovel; Dr. Beer hesitated, lingering over the sight, then joined me in the work.

A few years earlier we had an architect friend build the studio for us, mainly to have more space for our books. It looks like a shoebox proportioned according to the golden section. The walls all round are of glass, the beech wood bookshelves support the roof which is covered with earth, so that grass and poppies grow on it in the summer. To tell the truth, it's a criminally expensive storage room. When Oliver or Lorenz come to visit from Vienna, they sleep out there. Their boyhood bedrooms in the house have been repurposed as an ironing room and a library. Undine and her kids ignore the studio, don't even want to look inside. For Undine, our house is still her real home. She prefers to sleep in the bedroom she had as a child. Paula entered the garden studio only once, when she wanted to play me some Joe Zawinul tapes she'd brought from Vienna and the only stereo with a functioning cassette deck was out there. That same day, I drove to a reading. It was a Wednesday. On Friday she had her accident. I keep daydreaming that she comes to visit us with Philipp, her last boyfriend. In my dream they have a child, a girl named Emma, and when they come, we make a bed for her and Philipp and Emma in the studio and we fill the refrigerator with good things, and then I just can't remember which things she liked best to eat . . .

Whenever we have guests, which we seldom do, they sleep in the studio. Everyone's liked it up to now. The atmosphere and the light are magical and it smells of pine pitch. The magic doesn't work on Monika and me; it didn't work on Dr. Beer either. He asked if we were going to insist on banishing him from the house. Whereupon Monika made up the bed in Oliver's old room.

The work exhausted me sooner than I expected. He was clearly in better shape. He uttered a deep grunt at the toss of each shovelful, as though he'd always welcomed it—the battle with nature. I observed his face in silhouette, backlit from the neighbor's house. Some light reached us from the streetlight as well. Before the three of us had set off on our little walk, he had changed into rugged beige corduroys held tight to his ankles by bicycle clips so they wouldn't get wet, the kind of plaid pullover the English are fond of wearing, waterproof and whiskey-colored, and the aforementioned hat of kangaroo leather. We would be soaked with sweat by the time our work was done, but that made no difference. He was sure to have enough clothes in his suitcase to change again for dinner.

"Why haven't you ever told me about your wife?" he panted. "Everything I know about her I've heard from other people."

"From whom?" I asked.

He just shrugged.

3

The following morning we worked on my manuscript. Dr. Beer suggested we move out to the studio. He didn't want to sleep there, but it was O.K. for walking up and down and loud talking. The two rooms where I work are next to the living room and kitchen and obviously he didn't like the idea of Monika overhearing him playing the animal trainer and making me jump through the hoops of my own sentences.

We worked until twelve, then ate lunch in the kitchen with Monika: left-over rice pudding swirled in a pan with butter and cinnamon sugar, stewed plums from the freezer, and espresso. Then he put on his hat and set off on his walk. His hiking clothes had dried out on the radiator overnight. He slung a capacious knapsack over his shoulder. It was made of soft Provençal sheepskin, and he said he'd purchased it some time or other at Manufactum in Munich, behind the Rathaus. Evidently the only thing he used it for was to carry a notebook and pencil along on his walks.

"You look like Wilhelm Grimm," said Monika, "tramping off across the Hessian fields to look for someone to tell him a story."

"Wilhelm Grimm, of all people," he replied. "I'll always cherish the fact that you compared me to him. His brother is my great role model in everything I do."

Monika made him two ham sandwiches and filled a small thermos with tea. She told him that when he came to a double bench beside the path, he should sit down, take a breather, and admire the view of the mountains over in Switzerland while he had something to eat and drink. She promised he would remember that view when he'd forgotten everything else (by which she wanted to remind him of his visit to her jungle, because if there was anything he would *not* forget, it was that).

The foehn had let up a bit but was still blowing. At least it wasn't raining anymore. There were the typical corrugated clouds, with blue sky visible over the mountains to the south. The wind had melted a lot of snow during the night. It was as warm as May.

When we were alone, Monika asked if I wanted to walk across the Schlossberg with her since he had preempted my usual route. She hadn't been out on her mountain in three weeks and her spirits were low. She was determined to at least give it a try again today since she thought the foehn must have cleared away the snow up there, too. I told her to go ahead by herself and not worry about me. I'd answer my e-mails and read a bit or stretch out for a half hour or take a bath.

Since Dr. Beer had arrived, we hadn't had an opportunity to talk to each other alone. I would have liked to ask her what she thought of him, but since she didn't broach the subject herself I thought she didn't want to talk about him. She was enjoying the fact that he had fallen for her, and if we talked about it, maybe it would spoil her fun. She looked so beautiful; her dark hair shone and her eyes had an energy I hadn't seen for a long time. And it had been quite a while, too, since she'd worn those coarse weave army pants, frayed where they broke on her boots. On her they looked like an expensive item from some exclusive boutique.

When I caught sight of her from the kitchen window, riding her bicycle up our street that was free of snow at last (she'd leave the bike in the drugstore parking lot farther up the hill, at the base of the cliff), I knocked on the window and she waved her arm in good-bye without looking back over her shoulder.

I killed some time and ended up not answering any e-mails or reading or lying down on the couch or getting into the tub. I sat in front of my laptop for a quarter of an hour, ready to start writing. I replaced a light bulb in my room. That was about it.

I'd nodded off in my desk chair and started awake when Monika banged the garage door shut. She reported that she hadn't reached the top of the mountain. The path was still buried in snow and impassable beyond the last switchback.

Then Dr. Beer returned from his walk. He was in high spirits, happy; he hugged Monika, took her face between his hands, and his eyes filled with tears. He'd been gone three hours.
And had returned with a story.
"An unbelievable story!"
He started telling it even before he got his boots off.
As he was walking along the path I'd described to him, the one beside the autobahn, he'd seen a dog in the distance.
"It's happened to me on walks before. Usually there's no problem. I just call to the owners to put their dog on a leash. There are always a few of them out to prove something, but most are friendly and so are their dogs, probably."
This dog had no owner.
Footnote: he was afraid of dogs. He'd been afraid of them since childhood. He didn't know why. There wasn't any reason, no traumatic experience, for instance. Dogs sensed it, of course. Once, a dog expert had explained the chain reaction in a dog's brain: the dog smells your fear and knows—whatever "knows" means in a dog—how he would react if he were afraid, namely, if flight was still possible, he'd run. If it wasn't, he'd attack. And now the dog projects this pattern onto the human: here's a man who's afraid. It's too late for him to run; he's too close. He can't run as fast as me, the dog, so he's going to attack. Watch out! Once flight is no longer a possibility for the dog either, he'll preempt the human attack with one of his own.
"Ever since that dog expert explained how it works to me"— Dr. Beer laughed excitedly and a little hysterically and paused to

expel the air in his lungs, for he'd gotten so out of breath he couldn't get on with his story in whole sentences anymore, just one word at a time—"ever since I know all about it, it hasn't made me any braver. Not until today, that is. From now on, I won't ever be afraid of dogs again."

The dog made no move to run away when it saw Dr. Beer. On the contrary: it ran toward him. It was about thirty yards from him at first and the nearer it came, the faster it ran, as if it had been waiting for him. Dr. Beer stopped in his tracks, hoping the owner would turn up from somewhere. That was very unlikely, however. He had an open view of the surroundings: to his left was the autobahn beyond a chain-link fence; there weren't any trees or bushes growing there. To his right, between the path and the wooded bottom land along the Old Rhine, there was a large field that was at present a clean white expanse on which even a sparrow would have been visible from a great distance.

When the dog had gotten to within a few yards of him, he tossed his rucksack (the sheepskin one) over the chain link fence, clambered after it, and landed in the snow on the other side.

He waited for the dog to come up to him.

"I don't know anything about dog breeds, do you?"

A few years ago we had had cats. The last one was named Pnin, after the professor in Nabokov's novel which Monika happened to be reading when it showed up on our doorstep. Pnin was Lorenz's favorite; she slept on his bedspread. One day she disappeared. Friends advised us to get a dog. It would like living with people who went for walks so often and it would be good for us, too—like an everlasting child, so to speak . . . in our imagination perhaps, but only in our imagination.

"No, we don't know anything about dog breeds either," I said.

"Dachshund, spitz, German shepherd, pit-bull terrier, Rottweiler, Doberman, Appenzeller, Bernese mountain dog, Saint Bernard, and cocker spaniel," said Monika coquettishly.

It was a large black dog with a broad back, short-haired, brown spots on its head and a little bit of white, too. And it had a long, sturdy, powerful tail. It came up close to the fence and stopped where Dr. Beer was standing. It barked softly and wagged its tail. Only a little at first, but very energetically when Dr. Beer squatted down in front of it.

Dr. Beer said, "I'm afraid of you. Should I be afraid of you?" And he said it again, slowly and with exaggerated emphasis, as if the dog was a foreigner. "Should I be afraid of you? Should I be?" And then more and more quietly, until he was only moving his lips.

The dog smacked its lips and yawned, danced around, lowered its head, stretched out its front legs as if it were bowing, growled—but it sounded more like a murmur, at least it wasn't an angry growl—yawned again, looked away, narrowed its eyes to slits. But it behaved like that only as long as it heard Dr. Beer's voice; as soon as he was silent, the dog got to its feet and stood there quietly with its tail wagging slowly back and forth.

There was a steady drone of traffic from the autobahn. No one was in sight on the path or the field or on the other path that ran along the edge of the woods.

"Who do you belong to? Where's your master? Where's your mistress? Or are you out for a walk alone?"

The dog yawned again, licked its nose, did a dance with its paws.

"Go home! Leave me alone! I'll leave you alone too. You go that way, I'll go this way. I don't know where your master is—or your mistress."

He straightened up and waded through the wet snow by the fence. The dog sat down as if on command. When Dr. Beer turned to look back, he saw that the dog was watching him. He stopped; the dog didn't move. He called—called something like "Hey!"—and the dog ran to him.

"I'm not your master, so don't act like I am! I don't want to be. There's no point in obeying me. Go away or stay, but do what you want to, not what I tell you to!"

He recalled the smart dogs from the TV shows of his childhood: Lassie, Rin Tin Tin. In almost every episode, they had to race for help over stones and brambles, through streams and forests and then had to struggle to make the dull-witted humans understand that one of their species was in great danger somewhere and needed to be rescued. Man dumb, dog smart. And often: man bad, dog good.

"What happened to your master? Are you trying to tell me something? Or are you just waiting for me to climb over the fence so you can bite me in the leg?"

Dr. Beer was unable to discern any sign of aggression in the dog. But then, what did he know about canine physiognomy and body language? When a dog wags its tail—this much he was pretty sure of—it means "I'm happy." And this one here was wagging its tail. But it had powerful jaws, its legs were muscular and so were its shoulders, and its paws were like lion's feet with forbidding brown nails.

This time when he started to walk again, the dog followed him immediately and stayed so close to the fence that its flank was touching the chain link. Dr. Beer kept near the fence too. They walked along beside each other as if they did it every day. Whenever the man started walking faster, so did the dog. Whenever the man said something, the dog lifted its head and looked at him. They were like master and dog except that there was a fence between them that the dog couldn't cross. And then the man lost his fear.

After a while, the path diverged from the autobahn and the fence followed the highway. It had been installed to keep deer, rabbits, foxes, cats—or dogs—from straying onto the lanes and possibly causing an accident. Without the least sign of hesitation, the dog left the path and followed the fence, i.e., followed the man.

So the man squatted down in front of the dog again. This time, he stuck his fingers through the fence and wrapped them around the chain link. He hadn't dared to do that before. He'd been afraid the dog would snap at his hand. But the dog only sniffed it. Its nose touched his middle finger. The man was proud because he wasn't afraid.

"The way you look, I should be afraid of you," said the man. "But I'm not afraid. Still, it would be better if you went away. I don't know what to do with you."

Their noses were now close together. And for the first time, the man looked the dog in the eye. The dog was so close he had to squint. The dog expert had warned him never to do this: never look a strange dog in the eye, at least not for long, because they take it for pure aggression. The man looked the dog in the eye for a long time, and the dog looked back and wagged its tail. But then the dog turned its head away and licked its nose.

"Now," said the man to the dog while he straightened back up, "I'm going to climb over the fence. Don't hurt me!"

He went a little farther and the dog followed. He found a willow tree that had grown into the chain link fence. Its trunk had engulfed one of the transverse wires so it looked liked it had bored right through the wood. At that spot, the man climbed over the fence.

Before he dropped down on the other side he said "Don't hurt me!" again, and "Don't be afraid, dog!"

Then he jumped down right in front of the dog's face. When he landed, he stumbled to one side and twisted his ankle. It hurt, but only a little. The dog barked and wagged its tail so enthusiastically that it had to brace its hind legs so as not to lose its footing. The man put his hand on the dog's neck and stood up.

"What'll we do now?" he asked. "Shall I take you somewhere? Would you like that? There's nowhere I have to go. I can take any path. I've never been here before, so it all looks the same to me. You lead me wherever you want to go. We can walk together for a while."

But the dog remained sitting by the man's side, waiting for him to show the way.

"Are you hungry?" asked the man. He'd hung his rucksack on the willow before he climbed over the fence. He unbuckled the straps and took out one of the ham sandwiches. He gave it to the dog. It ate greedily—both ham and bread—and it would have liked more, but the man wanted to keep the other sandwich for himself.

It made the man very happy that the dog had let him put his hand on it and that he'd had the courage to do so, and he was touched—by himself and by the dog sitting next to him as if he were its master and had been its master for a long time. He bent down and stroked its head. The dog pressed its head against the man's hand and thigh.

"What shall I call you? You must have a name. Is it OK if I just call you 'Dog'? Dog, Dog, Dog," he said.

They followed the dog's tracks back to the path. They were alone. Far and wide there was no one else in sight. The man resumed his walk along the path; the dog walked beside him.

The man discovered that the dog wanted to stay on his right side. Whenever he circled behind the dog, it quickly took its place again on his right. For a while he played changing sides with the dog. The man came to the conclusion that this game neither pleased nor annoyed the dog. It was more like the dog didn't even realize it was a game. So the man stopped playing. But he kept talking to the dog. Even though he knew next to nothing about a dog's facial expressions he had no doubt that the dog liked it when he talked.

They came to a place where a narrower path diverged from the tarred main path and ran along an embankment. That's the way he should go, they'd told him, if he wanted to get to the double bench. The embankment led to a parallel path and it would certainly be cleared of snow. The snow was still deep on the embankment. The tracks of previous walkers were holes into which he sank up to mid-calf. The dog wouldn't be able to walk beside him here. It ran ahead, ran beside the holes, sank into slushy snow so deep in some places it had trouble struggling out again. Nevertheless, the man didn't turn back. Maybe the dog will get tired of this and leave me to go on alone. But he hoped it wouldn't.

When they got to the double bench, the man gave the dog the other sandwich to eat. He made do with the tea for himself.

The man sat on the bench and looked at the Swiss Alps across the way, as had been recommended. Far out in a field there was a tall, stately fir tree. Its south side was dark and free of snow, its north side rigid and white.

Attached to heavy wooden posts sunk in the ground beside the path were signs with pictures of animals and plants which walkers could observe in the area. The man learned that a tree frog native to this region was the only local amphibian that could climb trees and reeds in search of prey. He examined the painting of the great crested newt; it had a serrated comb all the way down its back and looked like a dragon. He read little commentaries about the great diving beetle, the water needle, and curly pondweed, about radican sword, devil's bit scabious, and a butterfly by the name of "Scarce

Large Blue (*Phengaris teleius*)." He wrote down the names in his notebook.

While the man read the signs, the dog sat by the bench.

"You're not worried I'll go away," said the man, "you wouldn't let me leave, would you?"

He caught sight of the dog's pink genitalia with their darker blotches and saw that it was a female.

He recalled that from one summer to the next he had ceased being a child. There was something he hadn't finished by the end of that summer vacation—for all the world he was unable to remember what it could have been!—and he'd resolved to finish it the next summer. But a year later, it had lost all importance and he'd forgotten about it—until today. Was it something that had to do with an animal, something that could only be done on vacation?

A jogger came running along the path. When he saw the man with the dog, he pulled up and ran in place. He waved to the man.

"Could you please hold onto your dog?" he called.

The man took the dog by the collar and drew it toward him. He put his other hand on its back. The jogger thanked him and ran past.

"He thinks you're my dog," said the man.

Then they continued.

They reached the gravel plant and the road that leads to the Swiss border. In just a few minutes they reached the customs shed.

The customs officer also waved to the man and called out, "Keep hold of your dog!"

The man took hold of the dog's collar and said, "It ran up to me on my walk. I don't know what to do with it. It's not my dog."

He could see that the customs officer didn't believe him. And he could see that he was afraid of the dog.

"I don't know anything about that," said the customs officer. "What can I say?"

"What should I do with it? It walks along beside me and acts as if I'm its master."

"That's hard to believe," said the customs officer.

"I couldn't have imagined it either."

"It looks mean."

"It isn't. Quite the opposite."

"That's what they all say."

"It really isn't."

"How do you know it isn't mean if it's not your dog?"

"It isn't dangerous. Not at all. It's been walking along beside me for an hour. You can pet it. Go ahead and pet it."

"I'd rather not."

"Go ahead! It won't do anything. I'm afraid of dogs too. More than you, I bet. But I'm not afraid of this one at all."

The customs officer took a step toward the dog.

Then the dog started to bark. The man had a firm hold on its collar. The dog reared up and growled and snarled and barked. It had a deep, adult voice and sounded very determined. But still, the man wasn't afraid of it and was surprised that he wasn't.

"Sit!" he cried, "sit!"

The dog sat down and stopped barking and the man thought, Now I've given myself away because why would the dog obey me if I'm not its master?"

The customs officer had run into his shed. He opened the window a crack. "Keep going!" he called.

"But where should I go?" the man called back. "I just don't understand it. It was friendly to me. I don't know what's wrong with it."

"My God, that's what they all say!" the customs officer rebuked him and shut the window and the man could see him still grumbling inside his little shed that looked so cozy from the outside.

Man and dog turned back. They came to a riding stable. Horses stood in the paddocks, motionless as statues. The man again took the dog by the collar and walked up to the barn. He could sense that the dog didn't feel comfortable here. Not that it strained at the collar, it only held back a little. Maybe this is its home, thought the man, and the dog doesn't want to go back here because it was abused. No, he thought, that would be literature.

"Is anyone here?" he called. "Hello? Is anyone at home?"

Two girls emerged from the barn. When they saw the dog, they crowded close together and pressed up against the barn door which was only open a crack.

"Is this your dog?" asked the man, although of course he knew it wasn't.

The girls shook their heads and disappeared. After a few moments, a man in blue overalls came out of the barn.

"Yes?" he asked. He gave the impression of being ready to defend himself.

"Does this dog belong to you?"

"What gives you that idea?"

"It started following me." He could tell that the man in blue overalls didn't believe him either. "No, he really did start following me. Perhaps you can help me out. I'm not from around here. I just wanted to take a walk."

"Some people get a dog," said the man in overalls, "and then when they have a dog they don't want it anymore, and then they bring it to a farm because they think it'll have it good there."

"That's not how it is. What I said was the truth."

He knew this man was not going to help him. So he walked back up the little slope to the path.

There he let go of the dog again. The dog went over to his right side. It pressed against the man's thigh and looked up at him. It made the man happy.

"You're a good dog," he said. "You protected me. The customs man wanted to harm me, the two girls wanted to harm me, and the man in blue overalls wanted to harm me too. You're a good dog. I like praising you. But I don't know what to do with you. And you wouldn't know what to do with me. And I don't have any more food for you. Run away! Or stay here! Go, run away! Or stay here!"

Then he thought, I'll figure out later how to get rid of it. Right now, I want to keep it for a little while.

And that was the story.

"We traipsed around a little longer," Dr. Beer continued, "walked across the meadows through the snow to a deer stand and then down to the water. Then we cut back through the woods along the river and finally reached the path again and continued back along the autobahn where the dog had run up to me three hours before. And then, at the autobahn underpass, it stopped dead. Wouldn't go another step. Wouldn't look at me anymore. Licked its nose and sat down and turned its head away—deliberately—and laid its ears flat. Cautiously, I kept going. Through the underpass. Didn't turn around to look at it. One step after another. In a second, I thought, it'll be back at my side. But it wasn't. I was already a good way into the tunnel before I finally looked back. It was still sitting in the middle of the path, still had its head turned away, wasn't following me with its eyes. Just imagine, it was completely ignoring me as if there hadn't been anything between us, for heaven's sake! So I kept going, what else? Maybe it's still sitting there. But what was I supposed to do? What would I have done if it had come running after me?

He looked at Monika.

"Would you have taken it in, a big beast like that? What would you think of a guest who brought you such a present? You'd say:

Thanks, but no thanks. It would have wrecked your jungle. Does a real monster belong in your jungle? Can it possibly have mistaken me for someone else? It occurred to me that it might have been traumatized. Maybe its owner had shoved it out of the car onto the shoulder of the autobahn and it was in shock and I was the first person it ran into after the shock. I think that's what must have happened. It found a hole somewhere in the fence and ran onto the path and just then I emerge from the underpass and it sees me and in its desperation its nerves and instincts get all mixed up and from then on, in its muddled brain, it belongs to me. And when we got back to the autobahn underpass it realized it wasn't my dog after all and the whole affair was embarrassing. That's my interpretation. What do you think?

Again, he addressed the question to Monika.

"It wolfed down your lovely ham sandwiches. I'm hungry!"

He left us no time to comment on his story or ask any questions or answer his. To celebrate the day, he said, we should please show him that "interesting" restaurant—his treat on the publisher's tab.

So I called up Martin Griesser, chef and owner of the Adler out on Kaiser-Franz-Josef Strasse, reserved a table for three in his extra room, and then called a taxi. Martin's an old friend and his place really is interesting—both interesting odd and interesting remarkable. The public rooms are furnished in the timelessly dreary Formica typical of the Sixties, but when you go past the open kitchen to use the men's room, you suddenly find yourself in a world of marble, brushed steel, sand-blasted glass and computer-aided everything, like some futuristic temple in the Chicago Loop. It's just that for now, the splendor hasn't made it beyond the john and the kitchen.

Monika and I were not a bit surprised that Dr. Beer was ecstatic about the food and the atmosphere, and when Martin came by our table to ask how everything was, Dr. Beer immediately told him the story of the dog. And he told the story once again that same evening, this time to the couple sitting at the next table. And before I went to bed, I heard him in his room talking on the phone and from the few words I could catch, I suspected he was telling the story a fourth time, on his cell phone, to whomever.

And suddenly I felt like a prosecutor. As if Dr. Johannes Beer was betraying his own story. Betraying the man it had happened to, betraying the dog, but above all betraying us, the first ones to hear it. My annoyance was stronger than all the alarm bells warning me not to make a fool of myself.

4

That night the wind picked up again, not a warm wind this time. I couldn't get to sleep. Finally I went downstairs, closed the shutters in the library, and heated up a saucepan of milk in the kitchen.

Monika came down and sat with me. I stirred cocoa powder into the milk and added some vanilla syrup. We haven't been sleeping so well since Paula died. That is, we don't sleep through the night. Monika says she's gotten used to it. I haven't. I wake up and feel a weakness inside me and think: I don't have the strength left to sleep. Before, such a thought would have seemed paradoxical. Why would you need strength to sleep, when sleep signals the end of your strength? I can force myself to write, force myself to go for a walk, force myself to read. Every two months I force myself to put together my income and expenses for our tax consultant and when I'm talking to friends, I'm able to mobilize reserves of strength I had thought exhausted long ago. I feel just as capable of the give and take of conversation as before and when I was shoveling the snow off the studio roof with Dr. Beer I soon got my second wind and was keeping up, shovel for shovel, and even looked forward to being stiff the next day. I can hike for five, six, seven hours without a break . . . but I don't have the strength to sleep. Don't stay in bed when you wake up, Monika says. Go downstairs, sit at the computer, surf Wikipedia, read something, turn on the TV or watch a DVD or listen to music or call someone up who can't sleep either. Just don't toss and turn in your bed; that's what wears you out! I've tried all that. With the help of Wikipedia and other websites I acquired a decent knowledge of medieval philosophy—I now consider myself an amateur specialist on the life and works of Johannes Scotus Eriugena and if I concentrate, I even think I can understand Anselm of Canterbury's proof of God's existence. I spend my nights ordering the relevant secondary literature from the central on-line catalogue of antiquarian books and the mailman brings them a few days later, alien objects that only begin to dispense their consolation once night falls again. Johann Sebastian Bach provides the soundtrack for my still, dark, cramped study—for many nights in succession I've listened over and over again to pieces from *The Art of the Fugue*, trying to fathom that gigantic web of double, triple, quadruple and mirror fugues and canons at every imaginable transposition interval. Each time the music desensitized me just a tiny bit more. At night, I don't envy the person I am during the day; but during the day I dread the night person a little. He has completely different needs, different thoughts, a completely different rhythm—everything a bit duller, more logical, more mystical, more medieval—which by the following day appears to be nothing more than a manifestation of my weariness.

"Don't try to change it," Monika says. "It's a good thing. It's your way. I have my way and you have yours." And yet—sometimes panic sinks its claws into my chest and hammers in my ear: you'll never sleep again like you used to, never again. And it sounds like Poe's raven cawing, "Nevermore! Nevermore!"

When nothing else helps, I crush half a Xanor—or a whole one—between a tablespoon and a teaspoon and wash the powder down with a glass of water. I'd rather just smoke like I used to. For a few years I've been taking Trittico on a regular basis; it's not addictive. I have respect for Xanor. I found a self-help group on the Internet where a woman writes that she swallows up to twenty tablets a day. She's tried to quit several times, but it was hell. She didn't make it, nobody can help her, she's given up all hope, and she'll probably kill herself. She really wrote that! Or else somebody thought it would be a good joke, some other lonely citizen of the Insomniac Republic with a copy of Dante's *Divine Comedy* in his hand and a finger in the *Inferno*. Some psycho-werewolf. To deal with his suffering, however great it was, he invented an even greater suffering and put it up on the Web. As bait. Despair seeking despair. Come, smell how sweet it is! – Our friend who ran the drug clinic for many years says that withdrawing from tranquilizers is really hellish, much harder than heroin.

Monika also got a prescription, a new medication for depression. At first, she suffered frightening side effects she couldn't precisely describe. Then after two weeks everything was fine. To help her sleep our psychiatrist prescribed Trittico for her too—a third of a tablet in the evening. I take two whole ones every day: a third in the morning and five thirds before bed. She bridges over the wakeful hours of the night by writing in her notebook—in a distinctive hand as astonishing and mysterious as her voice. I don't know what she writes; she doesn't read it to me.

And sometimes we meet in the night, in the kitchen, as if arriving from two different countries. Then I make cocoa for us. Monika cuts up a banana and gives half to me. One of us leans their head on the other's shoulder. Monika says she didn't dream about Paula again; I say I didn't dream about her either. Monika warms her hands on the mug and puts her feet in my lap for a massage. I do it because it reminds us of Paula. Paula used to lie on the couch in front of the TV and say: Rub my feet for me, Mama. It's the same with the cocoa. I made her cocoa for her heartache. She wouldn't sleep in her childhood bedroom anymore. When she visited from Vienna, Monika spread sheets and a blanket on the living room couch for her. The last time she slept in her own bed was just before her then boyfriend left her. She said that all their phone calls still haunted her room and made her feel ashamed. When she got back from Mexico she sat down at her computer and typed up the stories she had written down in a thick American high school notebook while traveling. During the day, she said, her room was a neutral space, even a bit alien, which she liked. At night it reminded her too much of the person she'd been. But even during the day, the door had to stay open.

Going for walks helps maintain our equilibrium somewhat. Monday through Friday we go our separate ways, Monika over the Schlossberg and me along the Old Rhine as far as Lustenau. On Saturday Monika comes along on my walk; on Sunday I go along on hers. No more alcohol, no more cigarettes either. Occasionally we go to the members' day at the Jewish Museum on the first Tuesday of the month; sometimes we're invited to literary or musical events (and afterwards always vow to go out more in the future); nicest are the evenings at the Adler with our rock musician friends. Afterwards we stink of smoke and our stomachs hurt from laughing. TV almost never—*Who Wants to Be a Millionaire* with Armin Assinger since it doesn't require any cathartic effort. We talk to Oliver, Undine, and Lorenz on the phone. We set it on speaker and place it in front of us. Oliver tells us about Marile, that he's bought her a strawberry-red ukulele and how amazingly well she can keep the beat. Undine passes the phone right on to Oskar or Soffie because she knows their little voices will lift our spirits and sharpen our memories. Before Soffie started school, she often visited us for a week or two, even for three weeks once, the little princess. Lorenz tells us about young women giving him the eye and about the painting he's working on at the moment. Next to the telephone there's a photograph of him with long hair, smiling, his head tilted to one side. He's painted a series of pictures of his sister who died. Two of them hang in our living room, one up front where the dinner table stands and the other above the couch in a corner, partially separated from the rest of the room. The power of her judgment pours from her eyes like pure, molten metal.

I've banished the instrument of the devil to the remotest corner of the bottom drawer of my desk: the digital blood-pressure monitor. At some point, I found an Internet forum where hypertension junkies exchange information, people who measure their blood pressure ten, twenty, thirty times a day. There were weeks when I was keeping right up with them. Well, this too is an illness, I thought, and decided to reconcile myself to the unmonitored risk of a heart attack or stroke. I also believe I've escaped another snare of the devil, namely the compulsion—every time I feel a little twinge—to search the Internet for self-help forums of people who suffer from little twinges. In the meantime, I'm doing better. I'm playing the guitar again. I couldn't for a long time after Paula died. Sometimes Paula and I would sit on the stairs and harmonize Dylan's *I Shall Be Released*. "Play it as a reggae," she would say. She accompanied me on tambourine. She did it to please me because she knew how much I like Dylan . . . Instead of accessing websites with health information or hooking up with discussion groups for neurotics and hypochondriacs, I look at sites with vintage jazz guitars: old Dobros, Nationals, Fenders, and Gibsons—a mild medication that trusts in the healing power of old dreams.

Every day we visit Paula's grave. Monika in the morning and I in the evening. On the weekend we go together. We see to it that the votive candles don't go out. We talk to her, each of us alone. Monika says good-bye by putting a finger on Paula's picture. I do it by putting mine onto the ground where her head is resting, the head I took between my hands so often when she was a child, but later too: the last time when I picked her up from the train at seven-thirty in the morning. She ran to me with outspread arms. The station master laughed and said he wished someone would greet *him* that way.

The visits to the cemetery do us good. They are why I'm averse to going on extended reading tours. Dr. Beer had said I would have to discuss that with the publicity department, it wasn't his responsibility. He'd be satisfied if they printed only two copies of every book he edited: one for the author and one for him. I did *not* say to him: Since our daughter died I'd rather not be away from home for so long. I said, "*Lately* I'd rather not be away from home for so long." I had hoped he would ask: Since your daughter died? And I would have answered: Yes, since Paula's death. I had hoped he would ask: Would you like to talk about it? I would have answered: Yes, I would. All our friends have asked at some point if we want to talk about Paula's death.

It's hard for me to walk over the Schlossberg with Monika. That's never going to change. We go past the place where Paula and her girlfriend slipped and fell. Her friend survived with a few abrasions. Paula hit her head on a rock. She was never really in this world, Monika says, only her toes had contact with the ground.

Monika went right back to bed after she drank her cocoa. I stayed in the kitchen and opened the *Standard* to the page with the sudokus. Sudokus had been another of the secondary manifestations of my depression—checking my blood pressure, *The Art of the Fugue*, solving sudokus. One entire summer long I watched for the *Standard* each morning. I didn't care about articles on politics or culture and I never read the business section or the sports pages anyway.

It was shortly after 2:00 and I hadn't even completed a first square when I heard someone on the stairs and thought, Monika's coming back down.

It was Dr. Beer.

He was barefoot and had on bottle-green pajamas with tiny rust-red diamonds and elegant lapels under a matching robe. They were either tailor-made or purchased cheap from China. Had he really brought along a robe for the two or three days he was going to spend with us? Was he perhaps allowing for the possibility that the three of us would breakfast together in our pajamas (which we then really did)? Or was the robe only for the trip from his room to the bathroom: two steps down and two steps back up? How many pieces of luggage would this man have needed for a two or three-week trip?

I asked if we had been too loud, which we certainly hadn't; Monika and I had hardly exchanged two words.

He said he couldn't sleep.

"Always, or just tonight?" I asked in the definite hope that this might set in motion a conversation between experts. I was at pains to eliminate a cold undertone from my voice. I wasn't entirely successful. (The prosecutor still lurked within me. But Dr. Beer had apparently exhausted his story; no mention was made of it and it stayed that way for the rest of the night).

"Just tonight," he said.

He seemed wide awake, refreshed, looked good, really good: his narrow, sun- or studio-tanned and clean-shaven face (had he shaved before going to bed?), his thick, aluminum-gray hair, cropped short all round, his slender hands with the well-formed, carefully manicured nails I'd noticed the first time we ever met. He wore neither watch nor ring. Even his feet were tanned, as if he was just back from a vacation in Sharm El Sheikh. He didn't use glasses.

He'd been reading, he said, browsing the mysteries shelved in his room. "You saved all your James Hadley Chase novels? I threw mine away, and Mickey Spillane and Earl Stanley Gardner too. Even Dashiell Hammett and Raymond Chandler. I used to read stacks of them when I was a student: Highsmith, Ambler, threw 'em all away. I burned most of them in the fireplace. A book is like a briquette."

I poured him a cup of cocoa.

He nodded back and forth a little. He had some music in his head and I was left to speculate what it was. I consider it a symptom of resignation that lately I feel myself more drawn to classical music while my old companions—Van Morrison, Bruce Springsteen, Neil Young, and all the others—no longer evoke the old stories in me, or maybe those stories no longer supply the energy needed to install myself and my life within them. He nodded as if he were listening to the blues. I would have liked to be there with him. He had returned victorious from the struggle with nature and was now at peace with mankind, confident that people would understand his story. It most assuredly did not encompass all aspects of his past, but he had told it and that sufficed: a man and a dog. With his toes he wiped a drop of cocoa from the floor. He sipped with pursed lips because the cocoa was very hot. He blew across the surface that wrinkled into a skin, then fished out the skin and put it into his mouth. That's just how I do it, always have. We loved the same books—a great part of what we possessed from the past bore witness to imaginary lands and imaginary towns where we had spent imaginary time with imaginary men and women, and it was often the same lands, towns, men, and women. And yet, just like two days ago on the telephone: I heard, he heard, how he, how I tinkered with a sentence—this time to call each other back and remind ourselves that we had been on the way to becoming friends, if such a thing is even possible at our age. If such a thing is still possible at our age, then certainly not out of the youthful power of sentiment, but rather as a decision, a well-considered placement of an equals-sign between our weights. It's like a cushion-shot in billiards; that's the best metaphor for its complexity I can think of. Of course, when the man encounters the dog, you have to report it in simple declarative sentences. Neither one of us had learned what Joseph Conrad and Ford Madox Ford were so successful at: keeping silent in each other's company. He was an editor and knew that even to praise silence you need a voice.

Here is a conversation I would like to have had with him. (Storm, night, heath, a hut, Lear and his Fool):
"How can I write about the death of our daughter?"
"Do you want to write about it?"
"Yes, I'd like to."
"I think I know what the problem is. You're not sure if you want to write literature or just remember. Am I right?"
"I want her to be with me. And I have the hope that she would be nearer if I wrote about her."
"I'm convinced that's true. But if you write about her, it's literature, and then other considerations come into play, considerations that will rein in your wishes and hopes and may even bend them into something else, because you'll need dramaturgy to make it into a story. Wouldn't that be like a betrayal?"
"Such a word has no meaning for me when I'm thinking about her. Every night before I go to sleep I hope I'll dream about her. I don't expect a dream to subject itself to dramaturgy. I don't want her to be the only real thing moving about in an invented world among imaginary things. You understand what I mean?"
"No."
"That I don't want to write only about what she was like. That her life will end at the age of twenty-one in literature, too—I don't want that."
"What if you just simply write down your memories and don't think about anything else?"
"I don't need to do that. I might need to if I were alone. Monika and I are always talking about how it was. All our memories end in her twenty-first year. I want to write what could continue to be, so that it's outside of me, you understand?"
"Yes, I understand that. I think I understand it. Perhaps that's always the first impulse when someone sits down and starts to write a story."

"And I can look at it and read it aloud to myself. And other people see it too and say: It's true. Actually: It could be true."

"For me, this impulse would suffice as a complete theory of literature."

"Theories don't interest me."

"I know that. And they shouldn't, either. Don't even start in with them!"

"Sometimes she'd call up and I could tell by the way her voice sounded what she'd say next. She would ask if Mom was home and I would call Monika over and she'd say: Set the phone on speaker, I want to read something to you. And then she would read us a story. And afterward she'd say, 'But tell me the truth if you think it's Rimbaud-shit.' 'Rimbaud-shit' meant any excess of emotion. She told about herself in many of her stories, but not what she had experienced, what was behind her, but about things that could still be ahead of her. In those stories, she told her life in advance, not in some distant future, but sometimes just a few minutes in advance. In the stories I'm thinking up, she still falls down the mountain, but it doesn't matter, she just slides down. But there's also a story that goes like this: One day I happen to go up on the mountain too and I hear her calling. She's calling for me, I see her slip, and I stand there like a rock and catch her as she falls. I told myself this story in the first months after her death, when the thought was still within me, the stubborn thought that it could all be just a dream. I believe in literature just like you believe in literature, otherwise my life would have been a failure and so would yours, I assume, and how could we take, say, Grillparzer and his Life is a Dream *seriously if there weren't something like that in reality, too, or at least if there hadn't been something like that? Or any other fairy tale! Or when Alice goes through the looking-glass! Tell me another story!"*

"Jean Paul's Speech of the Dead Christ from the Cosmos, that there Is No God. *There, someone is also dreaming who then wakes up and the dream was terrible and he's glad he woke up."*

"The mountain isn't in the later stories. When Paula and Lorenz were children, we told them a story every night. The stories they liked best started with the alarm clock ringing and the day beginning, and this day was the same day they had just lived through. In my later stories the telephone rings and she

says, 'Set it on speaker phone!' But instead of reading us a story, she tells us how happy she is with Philipp and that she may be pregnant and that she'd like to have it baptized Emma if it's a girl and Fritz if it's a boy. Or she tells us she'd like to emigrate to Mexico. When she got back from Mexico, the first thing she said was: I'm definitely going back there again. And this story continues that she lives in Mexico with her family and we visit her there, Monika, Oliver, Undine, Lorenz, and I. But then that's too far from any likelihood and there's nothing more about that story that I can believe. She could be any random person. She brought me back a cassette of Mexican music. Since there isn't a single cassette player left in the whole house, I lost it. She brought Monika a Mexican Madonna. It's there in the jungle."

"She wouldn't sleep in her room any more."

"Who told you that?"

"Monika told me when she was making up the bed for me upstairs. She told me that when Paula came home for a visit, she always said she would sleep in her own bed again tomorrow, tomorrow for sure. She couldn't do it today, but tomorrow for sure."

"Monika told you that?"

"Yes, when you were taking a shower after we shoveled the snow from the studio roof. After she made up the bed for me, we sat in the red armchairs by her jungle and drank tea and talked. She told me that Paula said her room reminded her too much of the person she used to be. Monika would like to write about your daughter too. But of course you know that. That's what she told me."

"She's written a story about her."

"I know, she told me that too. And she told me that she writes in her notebook at night when she can't sleep."

"And she also told you what she writes?"

"She said her thoughts were always circling around that sentence of Paula's that her room reminded her too much of the person she used to be. That's what she thinks about. But now she's come to the conclusion that it only means her boyfriend broke up with her in that room. That's all there is to it, although that's already plenty. She told me that at first, she found significance *in every little remembered detail, every object Paula had held in her hand, every expression in a photo, every line she found on a piece of paper or in a notebook. Now she thinks that was unfair, unfair to Paula because in hindsight it deprives her short life of its normality."*

"And how did you react to that?"

"I said I agreed with her. She shouldn't worry about it, I told her, she should just tell it."

"And did she?"

"Yes. She told me about Paula's last day. You had had the big birch tree taken down, Monika said, and she had gathered up the branches that were scattered all over the yard and Paula was up on the terrace, sitting cross-legged on the table, and watching her. Then Paula's friend came to pick her up for a walk on the mountain. And then the two police officers came into the garden, a policeman and a policewoman . . ."

"Please stop."

"But both of you would have to write about that too."

Perhaps that's what he would say.

He pulled the newspaper over to have a look. "You do sudokus? That's not healthy."

"What's unhealthy about it?"

"It makes you depressed."

I felt myself flush, as if he'd caught me red-handed. He *had* caught me red-handed. My depressions were nonsense.

"It's the same thing as inventing limericks. Erich Mühsam wrote them in his depressive phases. It's the saddest kind of literature except for sonnet cycles, which are even worse. Your compatriot Josef Weinheber must have suffered from depression. Why would a rational person do something like that? Your mountains aren't healthy either; they're also like a wall without an opening."

I heard Monika coming down the stairs. She stopped at the kitchen door. He had heard her too and smoothly changed the subject, started speaking louder to make sure she heard every word, and I was certain she did understand every word, because otherwise she would have opened the door and come in to join us.

He said, "I would guess that at some time or other, probably at a very early age, Monika must have . . ." (for the first time he called her by her name in my presence and he did it so that she would know, out there on the other side of the door, that we were talking about her and not some random personal pronoun) ". . . looked in the mirror and realized that no matter what she did, no one would ever think she was an unattractive woman."

He waited until we could hear the stair treads creaking again, then he laboriously got to his feet—an effort I wouldn't have thought necessary from his firm, straight, muscular body—bent down to me, put his hands on my shoulders, hesitated a while, and at last said, "You two made me very happy this evening. Thank you."

He had found his sentence and I found mine. I said, "You would never let me get away with a phrase like that."

"Of course I wouldn't," he chortled and left the kitchen.

5

My misfortune happened on the third day of his visit. He wanted Monika and me to walk down to the Old Rhine with him (where I suspected he intended to tell us about his adventure again on location). Monika told us to go ahead without her; she wanted to give the Schlossberg another try: maybe the path would be more kindly disposed today.

"Why don't we come with you?" asked Dr. Beer.

She didn't want us to.

At this point, he couldn't revert to his principle of "going for a walk and being alone no matter what," at least not without insulting me, and I couldn't remind him of his principle, at least not without insulting him.

At the autobahn underpass I said—why, I'll never know—that I'd rather walk down along the Old Rhine than stay up here beside the autobahn. The sky was full of low-hanging clouds and the temperature was just about freezing. The tops of the pylons for the overhead power lines were indistinct against the featureless gray. A minivan with its lift gate open was parked by the allotment gardens. A man and a woman looked our way. He was carrying an armful of firewood and she had her hand on the door of their garden shed. I said hello and they nodded in reply. Dr. Beer waved.

The Old Rhine was still frozen but large puddles of water had formed on its surface. The foehn had melted away the snow and the path was spongy. Our boots sank into the slush up to our ankles, which didn't seem to bother my companion. Nor did it seem to bother him that we couldn't get a conversation going in the daytime, either. So we kept silent. As always, it made me uncomfortable to walk beneath the trees even though their crowns were bare and we could see the sky through their branches.

At first, the path was wide enough to walk side by side. At the ford it got narrower and led up into the wooded wetlands. I walked ahead. Alders, willows, and ash were growing up between the big stone blocks of the old dam; in some places their roots had forced the stones out of true. Branches had broken off beneath the weight of the snow and ripped long strips of bark from the trunks as they fell. Younger trees were bent down to the ground and it was slow going through the woods. Finally, we climbed back down to the water and walked past reeds sticking up out of the ice. There were no footprints on the path; we were the first walkers after the big snow. Over on the Swiss side, boys were skimming stones across the ice.

We had just rounded the first point of land where swimmers sunbathe in the summer—Swiss and Austrians harmoniously side by side—when I saw the dog, just as Dr. Beer had described it to Monika and me and the owner of the Adler and the couple at the next table and then to somebody else on his cell phone in the middle of the night: large, dark, with brownish-white spots on its head. It was standing out on the ice of a flooded gravel pit with its nose lowered to the surface. Dr. Beer was fiddling with his boot laces and hadn't spotted it yet and for a moment, I considered just taking him by the arm and telling him I'd had enough and wanted to go home.

But instead I said, "Is that it?"

"Yes, that's her!" he cried and ran out onto the ice with his laces still untied. "Dog! Dog!" he called in delight, "You recognize me? Come here, big girl, come!"

"Don't do that," I yelled to him.

The dog barked and set off at gallop. At first it couldn't get a foothold on the ice and its hindquarters slid and twisted sideways, but then it ran toward the man it had taken—and apparently still took—for its master.

And broke through the ice.

It broke through not far from the gravel bank. I knew this body of water well. It was shallow near the bank but only a few feet farther out the bottom had been dredged. Maybe it would have been possible for it to climb out of the water if it hadn't flailed its hind legs so wildly. That just made it sink in more. It braced its front legs on the ice but in a few seconds, its body was two-thirds under water.

Dr. Beer promptly ran back to shore, his legs far apart and his arms spread out to cover the largest possible surface area in case he broke through, which was completely pointless since every time he took a step he put his entire weight onto the tiny surface of one sole anyway. On his side of the pond, the side of the little inlet that was in shadow, the ice held. Willows, birches and pines arched their branches over the shore; even in summer, the path beneath them was seldom dry.

"What'll we do?" he called out before he reached me. He was out of breath when he finally came up. "She'll drown if we don't pull her out."

I ran around the shore of the inlet to a spot nearer the dog.

"Come on," I yelled, "*kommen Sie!*" (in the heat of the moment, I'd reverted to the formal *Sie*, and that made me want to laugh), "maybe she'll get out by herself."

I really did have to suppress a laugh too, because the dog looked so comical. She was wildly staring and struggling and panting so loud it echoed around the whole inlet. Any moment now she was going to pull herself out—I had no doubt of that. Far and wide, there was nothing to suggest that something terrible could happen here.

But she wasn't having any luck and we had to do something if we didn't want to watch her drown.

From a pine tree, Dr. Beer snapped a long branch as thick as his arm which the snow had already half broken off.

"She's a smart dog," he said. "She knows we're trying to help her. If she bites into the branch, we can pull her out."

But the branch wasn't long enough. We stood on the shore and pushed it out onto the ice, but it was at least two yards short of the spot where the dog was fighting for its life. And we didn't dare venture out onto the ice ourselves.

We looked around for another branch. A willow had split down the middle and it would have reached. We tried to tear a piece off but the wood was green and tough.

"Do you have your cell phone along?" he asked.

"No, of course not."

"I'll run back," he said, "maybe those people are still there, maybe they have a cell phone. The fire department comes right away in situations like this, at least they do in Frankfurt."

"Let me go. I know those people," I said. "You stay here. It's your dog."

"I can't," he said and took off without a word to the dog or even a backward glance.

My recollection of what followed is impaired, which doesn't mean I lack the details—quite the opposite! It's more that it's hard for me to separate the essential from the unimportant. In the situation I was in, everything was essential because I perceived everything around me as if for the last time. By impaired, I mean less the content of my memories than their form, the way they present themselves to me. In my recollection, a compassionate angel dissolves the boundaries of my sense of self and allows its edges to melt so that today I can no longer discover the person I was at that moment—except in a figurative sense, the way you discover within yourself a person from a novel whom you identify with. I see myself stepping to the edge, see the person I was putting his foot onto the ice. I hear the person I was speaking to the dog, encouraging it, telling it not to give up, promising it would be rescued—but it was also clear to him that he couldn't wait for help to arrive and had to do something without delay because the dog was getting tired.

He stepped onto the ice. It supported him. But bubbles appeared beneath the surface. That meant the ice was tipping up in one place and down in another. He jumped back onto the shore and went to try it from the more wooded side. The ice was thicker in the shadow of the trees. He walked out carefully, one foot in front of the other, and spoke to the dog in a calm voice. When he was within a few yards of it, he saw the dog's front paws slip and its head go under. He lay down on the ice then and crept as fast as he could toward the hole. He reached it at the same moment the dog's head emerged from the water. He stretched his arm out and the dog sank its teeth into his coat sleeve and didn't let go.

"That's good," he said. "Don't let go! I'm going to grab you now, so don't bite me!"

He put his free hand into the water and grabbed the dog behind one of its front legs and even succeeded in lifting it up a little. He braced his elbow on the ice, causing water to run into his sleeve; his glove already had water in it and it was even colder than he'd feared. Good thing I wore my coat and not my jacket, he thought. It was a quilted down coat that reached to mid-calf.

The dog was flailing its hind legs again and snorting loudly. That was good, but it was also dangerous.

"That's good," he said, "but don't kick too hard or you'll pull us both in."

Now he reached behind the other front leg. The sleeve the dog was biting got pushed back and water got into it too and seeped up above his elbow. I have to let her go he thought or I'll catch a cold, maybe even pneumonia. But he didn't let go.

He did let go with one hand, however, and took hold of the sleeve the dog had buried its teeth into and tugged at it, but the dog had bitten through the material and its jaws were clamped together. What if she goes under and drowns but doesn't let go of my sleeve, not even in death, he thought. Then I'd have to take off the coat. My house key's in the pocket, he thought.

The dog slid back into the water.

"You've got to help me," he said but he didn't know how she could help. "It won't be long before the fire department gets here."

Does the fire department here even respond to such calls, he thought. And what if the man and woman with the allotment garden had already gone home? It looked like they were just picking something up or dropping it off. What would keep them there at this time of year and in this weather?

I have to go it alone, he thought.

He tried to wriggle backwards. To do that he had to free up one hand. But that caused the dog's front legs to slip from the ice and its head went under again. Only its nose was still sticking out because it wouldn't let go of the coat.

"Put your paws back on the ice," he yelled at her.

The dog's weight was pulling on his arm. More ice crust at the edge of the hole crumbled.

"The best thing would be if you put your paws on the ice and otherwise keep still," he said. "We'll both just keep still and wait, that would be best. Someone will come soon."

The only thing to do was grab the dog's legs again and lift her out of the water. It was harder than before. Up to now he'd been able to keep his face and neck from touching the ice. Now the dog's weight pulled him down and water ran into his collar and the cold stung his cheek.

"Put your paws on the ice!" he yelled. "Put your paws on the ice, goddamn it!"

It sounded like a movie and he was amused.

As long as I feel like I'm in a movie, he thought, there's still hope that she'll be saved. And that thought amused him even more. What did those two things have to do with each other? But wouldn't it be nice if you could be sure that things would turn out all right whenever you could compare your situation to a movie? On the other hand, as a matter of fact, any situation at all could be compared to a movie, because movies had already been made about every possible situation. And at the same time, he was aware how crazy it was to be thinking such drivel in the present situation. It wasn't like him to be silly and he wasn't a fool either and he told himself I have to take such thoughts as a warning that I'm in more danger than I think—not just the dog—and I'm a human and she's a dog and it occurred to him that legally, dogs were still considered things and at the same time he realized that that thought was also crazy. I have to let go of this dog right now or else I'm done for, he thought. How will I ever get home this wet and frozen? It was a good mile and a quarter. If I run the whole way, he thought, then maybe . . . then for sure I can make it. I've done it before. Until not too long ago he had gone jogging three times a week, even when it was below freezing. He'd gotten completely sweaty every time but had never caught a cold. You just couldn't sit down to rest or go slowly. You had to produce more heat than the cold you were absorbing. I'll jog home, he thought, and get right into the tub and then I'll be OK.

He started to pray, "Our father, which art in heaven, hallowed be thy name. Thy kingdom come, thy will be done, send some help soon."

His thoughts distracted him from the dog. For a moment it seemed like he was alone on the ice. The dog had stopped moving.

Her paws lay on the ice and she wasn't moving anymore, just as he'd told her to do. Her eyes were wide open, looking at something or at nothing.

"Move a little," he said, "or you'll freeze. Just move a little bit is all."

Water had soaked into his coat and gotten through to his skin and for the third time he thought about letting the dog go. If she's dead, what's the point of keeping hold of her? She can take the coat and the house key with her for all I care. But the dog was still alive, her eyes hadn't dimmed. Her mouth sank into the water again and again and she didn't have the strength left to raise her head.

"Hey, are you cold?" he asked. At least he thought he'd said that to the dog. But he wasn't sure if he'd heard his own voice or just imagined it. And why would he have asked that, he wondered. Of course she was cold.

For his part, he wasn't so cold anymore since his chest, belly, genitals, and thighs were wet. That's not a good sign, he thought. My body is shutting down. Somewhere he'd heard or read—or had he come up with the theory himself?—that in extreme situations, the body hurried ahead of the mind, could see more clearly because it had no prejudices, not even a prejudice against death. At first it struggles against death according to its own plan because it can't depend on the plans of the intellect. But then, when it realizes there's no more point in resisting death, it starts shutting down all its functions and sensations to ease a person's dying. That's why I'm not so cold anymore, he thought, and now he didn't feel cold at all. It was as if he had forgotten what cold and heat were.

But I'm not dead yet, he exulted, and without any advanced warning the thought came to him that founding a religion is, strictly speaking, to take a first step away from God. And he thought, how lovely it would be to at least have enough time to think that through a bit more.

Again he prayed.

But this time not from desperation but from simple convention. And it put his mind at ease because it was as if instead of himself, the others were praying for him. The dog stared into his eyes. That's not a good sign either, he thought. One of a dog's instincts is not to maintain direct eye contact for too long. So her body is shutting down too. But that would mean that her instincts have already cleared the way for death. But it has to get past me first, he thought.

Not just his hands had lost all feeling, so had his arms. They wouldn't obey his commands any more. Even if I wanted to I couldn't let go of her now, he thought. She can't let go of me and I can't let go of her either. My coat and the house key have nothing to do with it. He rolled a quarter-turn onto his side and because his arms felt like they were screwed into his shoulders without a hinge in the middle, that had the effect of raising the dog an inch or so out of the water, and that was all it took.

The dog drew a deep breath and exhaled. Drops of water sprayed onto its nose.

"There you are again!" he said and this time he heard his own voice and didn't doubt its reality. "Can you still move your legs?"

Now he rolled to the other side and the dog's head broke completely free of the water. It flailed its hind legs again.

"That's right, kick your legs!" he said. "But not too hard, please!"

He heard a noise like wood splintering.

"Help!" he yelled. He wasn't sure if his cry was real or if he'd just thought it or dreamed it.

Then the ice broke beneath him.

6

I was screaming. That much I know. Or rather: something inside me screamed. And I know that I tried to hold fast by digging my fingernails into the ice. I could feel the dog's nails clawing at my back. She was trying to get out over my body. Her flailing legs pushed my head under water and my heart was heavy and so light.

But the men with the ladders were already there. They'd already been there before the ice broke. They had called to me but I hadn't heard them.

I didn't lose consciousness but my perceptual capacity was greatly reduced. I registered movements, must have known that people were around me, but I didn't distinguish their faces and couldn't understand what they were saying. They wrapped me in blankets and put me on a stretcher and took me to the hospital and in the hospital they wrapped me in foil so my body could thaw out gradually. I had deep gashes on the back of my neck from the dog's claws. In my condition, far removed from reality, I belonged more to the things floating before my eyes than to myself, and the dog's lack of gratitude pained me and I thought I'd never enjoy life again and I felt a dread I'd never felt before, namely, the dread of returning to life. But at the same time I was confident that this feeling would soon disappear like a sharp but transient pain and I would be greeted with open arms as I had been greeted three years ago at our train station.

That same evening, Dr. Beer and Monika came to visit me in the hospital. He squeezed my hand but I don't know if he said anything. I went right back to sleep.

When I woke up he was still sitting by the bed. He was alone. I didn't know how long I'd slept or if he'd gone back to our house in the meantime. I didn't even know how long I'd been there.

He said that Monika and he were spelling each other. I was going to be OK. In a few days I'd be fully recovered and it would all be just a bad memory. The dog was fine, too. He said they had taken her to a shelter. I was a celebrity for rescuing her and a regional newspaper had already requested an interview. He squeezed my hand again and held it for a long time.

"What should I do with it?" I asked.

"With what?"

"With this story."

At one point when I was in Frankfurt I had asked who his favorite hero in literature was. He'd thought in over for a moment and said, "Mister Verloc in Conrad's *The Secret Agent*."

"Verloc?" I exclaimed. "He's a devil!"

His reply: "Unfortunately, you put me into the awkward position of having to remind you that that story is literature, not life."

Whereupon I told him a story that was real life and not literature. In the train to Frankfurt I'd been in the dining car, watching a group of young people who were behaving like spoiled brats. One of them, a slim, blond, conceited young woman, was being especially brazen. She dropped her knife, ordered the waiter to pick it up, then dropped it again. Shortly thereafter, I reencountered her in the station. An older man had his arm around her shoulder and was talking urgently to her, their faces close together. An older woman was waiting a step behind them, her hands folded as if in prayer. The young blonde broke down. She cried out, wept, covered her face with her hands. Her screams echoed through the waiting room and she doubled over, her arms hugging her belly. Her mouth was despair, her eyes were despair, her body was despair. And I, I said to Dr. Beer, I was overwhelmed with sympathy and shame that only a few minutes earlier, I had wished all sorts of bad things upon her.

Dr. Beer had listened without expression.

"Is that the end of the story?" he asked.

"Yes," I said.

"Good," he said, "very good. If you write that story down, include a young man or woman who's not as bad as the others, someone who tries to get them to see reason. It would also be interesting to have another girl who rebukes the blonde, in order to highlight her impudence even more. But don't overdo it and give her black hair. In the second part of the story, instead of describing your own feelings, you could insert a succinct memory of your own, but not of a similar event—you need something that leaves room for associations . . ."

"I don't want to write the story down," I had interrupted him.

"Don't tell me things you don't want to write about! I'm your editor!" he had replied.

They kept me in the hospital for three days. That was unnecessary, of course, but I was the hero who had saved a dog's life and they assured me that heroes get special treatment. The wounds on my neck bothered me the longest.

Right after visiting me in the hospital, Dr. Beer had returned to Frankfurt. And then I got a letter in which he informed me that a younger colleague would be taking over the work on my manuscript.

Michael Köhlmeier
Madalyn

Translated by
David Dollenmayer

Translation © 2015 by David Dollenmayer

64

Chapter One

Madalyn hadn't yet turned fourteen in the spring of '09. I'd known her since she was born. When the Reises moved into our building in the Heumühlgasse, Frau Reis was pregnant with her. Herr Reis worked for a company that designed machines that made computer chips—machines that got built somewhere else, not in Vienna. He was an engineer or a manager or some combination of the two. It was said that both he and the firm still had some cards up their sleeves. I heard that through the building's rumor mill, which I enjoyed being part of, especially when the talk was about money and the future. It was a time when almost everyone was buying stock. I myself bought a million schillings' worth of shares in a Brasilian telecommunications fund; five years later they were worth barely a tenth of what I paid for them. Herr Reis and his wife invested more wisely: they bought the apartment on the floor below mine, which led me to assume they planned to stay. From my study window I had a view of their balcony. There was a silvery gray wooden bench and a little table whose surface was a mosaic of the head of Botticelli's Venus. I'd never seen anyone sitting there. One time, I found myself in the elevator with the very pregnant Frau Reis and since nothing else occurred to me (and it was also true), I told her that we were looking forward to her baby—all of us in the building—and I added that she'd have a great choice of baby sitters. She wasn't very talkative and afterwards I felt foolish for being so forward. Frau Malic, the main coordinator of all the gossip in the building, told me that the Reises belonged to some sort of Christian sect. I didn't want to hear about that. I was trying to resist my own curiosity and was succeeding very well. But I was to have a special connection to their daughter Madalyn, a friendship that lasted all through her childhood, and there was a reason for that.

For her fifth birthday, Madalyn got a bicycle. It was in the fall. She learned how to ride all by herself. Every afternoon after kindergarten, she would walk the bike across the Naschmarkt, go into the little park on the Linke Wienzeile, and then mount up and roll down its low, artificial hill. And I happened to be the first person for whom she demonstrated her newly-learned skill. Sometimes I would sit on a bench under the maple trees between the swings and the slides—actually, I only did so in the fall and winter when there weren't any children and the little park was also forsaken by grown-ups and, although in the middle of the city, it was as quiet as in the woods. So I was sitting there reading when Madalyn came along with her bike. Unlike her parents, she was talkative. She wasn't shy at all. In the stairwell, she'd already told me about her first day in kindergarten and continued to give me interim reports every time we encountered each other there. She showed me the paper airplanes she'd made in her creative play group and we flew them out the stairwell window and into the rear courtyard. She liked playing in the stairwell and she always played alone. She talked out loud to herself; the acoustics obviously appealed to her. Evelyn and I had often enjoyed eavesdropping on her. We liked her husky voice. It seemed to go with her wild, curly, unmanageable hair and her small face with its slightly coarse features. Evelyn said she reminded her of herself, and not just because both their names had the same last syllable. As a child, Evelyn had also played alone most of the time and, like Madalyn, talked to herself all afternoon long in conversation with an imaginary girlfriend.

Madalyn said she wanted to show me what she could do. She got on her bike and started off, shrieking and pedaling and riding in circles on the lawn. She still had trouble coming to a stop, however. She steered toward me and yelled to me to catch her. She was proud of herself because up to then, she'd only ridden without pedaling. I said that meant that from that day on, she really knew how to ride a bicycle, because if you can't pedal you don't really know how. You have to be able to pedal to call yourself a real bicycle rider. And during the next hour, with me as a witness, she also learned how to brake and come to a stop.

"Do I really know how to ride a bike now?" she asked.

"Just as well as the next guy," I said.

I shouldn't have been so positive about it. A few days later, without paying attention to the street, she zoomed out of the driveway of our building and right in front of a car. She was thrown fifteen feet and landed on the pavement. Which was fortunate, because she might have gotten caught under the wheels of the car like her bicycle. And by chance, I was again a witness to what happened. I was coming up the street from the Naschmarkt and saw it all. I ran over to her. The driver was sitting motionless in the car with her hands clutching the wheel and her eyes closed. Madalyn had lost consciousness. She was bleeding on the inner side of her arm, below the elbow. I didn't have my cell phone with me and called loudly for help. A man looked out of a window and I shouted to him to call an ambulance. "Dial 144! dial 144!"

Madalyn's arm was bleeding so heavily that a pool of blood was already forming on the asphalt. A piece of skin had been torn away on the inner side. I took off one of my shoes and bandaged her arm with my sock. She opened her eyes and when she saw me, her mouth twisted and she began to sob. I said it was all right, I was with her and her Mama would be there soon. In a few days she'd be laughing about it.

"I promise, Madalyn. I know what I'm talking about."

I didn't dare lift her up to a sitting position and put my arm around her.

By this time, a crowd had gathered, including a woman from our building. I told her to ring the bell of the Reis family and tell

Madalyn's mother what had happened. Her father was sure to be at work and not at home. Her mother wasn't home either.

The ambulance arrived and Madalyn was put on a stretcher. She kept a tight hold on my hand and asked me in a faint voice not to go away. The doctor said it would be okay for me to ride along. During the trip to the general hospital she never let go of my hand. I stroked her forehead while the doctor saw to her injuries. There was also a wound on her head that I hadn't noticed. I talked to her and strove to maintain a calm, ordinary tone of voice. Which I found difficult. She tried to smile, but the corners of her mouth soon turned down again and she started to sob and I had to control myself so I didn't start sobbing too.

Except for the wound on her lower arm, which no one could really explain, and a slight concussion, Madalyn had gotten off uninjured. They kept her at the general hospital until her mother could get there to pick her up; she didn't get there until that evening! They hadn't been able to reach her, and the same with Madalyn's father. At his company they said he was traveling to an important meeting and his cell phone was turned off in accordance with company policy. The doctor planned to give her parents a good talking to. He was even thinking of reporting them for child neglect, he said – leaving a five-year-old child alone from noon until evening! When Frau Reis arrived, he withdrew and left me to handle things.

She had an intimidating way about her, staring at you without moving a muscle as if she was frozen. I explained what happened and refrained from criticizing her. However, I did intend to come downstairs the next day and give her a piece of my mind. What had happened didn't seem to bother this woman too much. Nor did she thank me. I carried Madalyn out to her car. Frau Reis didn't even offer me a ride. I took the bus and subway home from the hospital. Everyone has their own way of dealing with shock, I thought, and this was Frau Reis's.

A few days later my doorbell rang. Madalyn was standing there with her arm and head bandaged. She was holding a drawing she had made for me. She had drawn the accident in a sequence of pictures.

"I wanted to thank you and I drew this for you."

"I like it a lot," I said. "I'm going to frame it and hang it on the wall."

"Really?" she said, "like a painting?"

"I think it's a work of art," I said. "And it tells a story too. Most works of art don't tell a story, but this one does."

The drawing was of our shared adventure. I was there too, in every frame. Me walking along the street and seeing Madalyn fly through the air; me squatting next to her on the ground with a lake of blood between us; me sitting in the ambulance with the Red Cross on its side and holding Madalyn's hand. I took the picture to Wolfrum's art shop next to the Albertina and chose a black lacquered frame with gold stripes. Once I had hung it on the only piece of empty wall in my library, I went downstairs. Madalyn was there by herself again. I said I'd like to invite her father and mother – and her too, of course – to tea or coffee or cocoa and show them the framed picture. She didn't want to wait for her parents; she wanted to see it right away.

Evelyn was completely smitten by the picture (at the time we were in the midst of discussing whether we were going to move in together), but most of all she was fascinated by the fact that Madalyn had addressed me with the formal pronoun *Sie*.

"That's really unusual," she enthused. "Her parents obviously put a lot of value on good manners."

"Obviously," I said.

From then on, Madalyn and I had even more to say to each other whenever we met on the stairs or on the street in front of the building, or in the courtyard while taking out the garbage. She told me about her first day of school, showed me her first report card and what she had gotten for Christmas. She described an excursion her class took to the Lainz Nature Preserve where they had seen wild boars and their young, and she was ecstatic in the summer because she had learned to swim and she told me how wonderful it was. Sitting on the windowsill in the stairwell, I once helped her with her math homework, and when she told me a joke, I laughed out loud with genuine amusement. When she asked if she could polish my shoes I said we'd do it together. "You polish yours and I'll polish mine." And so we sat on the stairs and brushed and polished and talked.

If I didn't see or hear her for a week, I got restless. More than once, I stood at the Reises' door with my finger already on the doorbell because I wanted to ask about her. Of course, I never pushed it. Since Madalyn's accident I had the impression that her mother was now not only monosyllabic, but actually avoiding me, which I could somehow understand. But more than that, I imagined that I saw reproof in her eyes. Even that was probably understandable, but it annoyed me nevertheless.

But Madalyn liked me, and it made me happy to read it in her face.

She once said to me, "You saved my life." I didn't try to contradict her.

"It was the most beautiful thing I've ever done," I answered.

Chapter Two

In the spring of '09, in late March, she stood at my door and was very ill-at-ease. I hadn't seen her for quite a while. I'd just returned from America a few days earlier. I went there for one reason only, namely, to breathe the air of hope again after eight depressing years of George W. Bush. I had lived there for almost two years in the eighties, after all, expecting to remain forever. I visited my friends Antonia and Lenny Redekopp in North Dakota. They were an old couple by now, but still active enough to campaign for the Democrat Barack Obama.

Madalyn was hugging a ring binder to her chest. "I'm probably disturbing you," she said.

"You never disturb me," I said.

"But I can come another time if you'd rather. I would have called beforehand but I didn't know your number and it's unlisted."

"Come in." And I stood aside to let her by. I didn't ask about her parents. She might have misconstrued it as me thinking she had to ask permission to do the slightest thing—although in fact, she did.

Even before she got her shoes off, she started in: "Lately we've been talking a lot about literature in school, especially Austrian literature, and I said I knew the writer Sebastian Lukasser and our teacher got all excited because you're so famous and I didn't even know that, and Mrs. Petri said I should ask if you would agree to let me interview you, and if you do and if it's good, I'll get a good grade."

Madalyn was in the eighth grade in the Gymnasium on the Rahlgasse. It was the nearest school to us—from the Heumühlgasse you go across the Naschmarkt, past Café Sperl (we often waved to each other through the window when she rode her bike past on the way to school while I was having breakfast)—a remarkable school, by the way. They had some homerooms that were all girls—Madalyn was in one of those. The principal was a "good feminist" Madalyn had told me on another occasion. Madalyn was a good student.

The interview wasn't a pretext, definitely not. We got through it perfectly well. I was flattered and told her so, but was concerned at the same time that the unselfconcious friendship we had enjoyed up to now might suffer from my "fame." I told her it wasn't that big a deal. I loaned her my old dictaphone, showed her how to use it, and promised to talk in short sentences so she wouldn't have so much work transcribing them. She had prepared a list of questions and read them out to me. First, why did I become a writer? Second, what was my typical day like? Third, which of my books was my personal favorite? I answered her questions and—partly to show off a bit—went on to say that after finishing my last book, which was very long and was really my favorite, I'd finally started working on a new novel. It was the story of a man who at the age of—"well, about your age, Madalyn, or just a little older"—had commited a murder and how the rest of his life had gone. Fourth, a question her teacher had asked her to ask me: what was the hardest thing about writing for me?

"*Who's* telling the story," I answered without hesitation. "Should the murderer himself tell it or an omniscient narrator, or should I, Sebastian Lukasser, tell it?"

"Is it a true story?" That question hadn't been in her notebook. "Do you know the murderer personally?"

"Yes," I said, "I know him."

She wasn't surprised in the least. "Wouldn't it be best for *you* to tell the story? You're doing it anyway. Why should you pretend someone else is?"

That made sense to me.

No, the interview wasn't a pretext. But I soon sensed that it was—at least could have been—an opportunity for her to get something else off her chest, too. And toward the end, when I started spouting long sentences after all, I could see that her mind was wandering and the dutiful nodding with which she responded to my explanations betrayed more restlessness than interest.

But she couldn't bring herself to talk about the other thing that was bothering her. At least not that day.

She came back.

The next day, right after school – she said she hadn't even been home yet – she was standing at my door with her backpack and this time, she didn't ask if she was disturbing me but walked past me into the hall, shutting the door behind her.

She had already written some questions and answers into her notebook and wanted to show them to me.

"I was still up in the middle of the night, listening to the tape," she said, and since she was so pleased by the phrase she repeated it immediately: "In the middle of the night I was still up working."

Her handwriting was very childish. She had written with a pen. I was moved. She had made intelligent choices about which answers to write down. I said I had no idea how she could make it any better.

"Then the interview is finished?" she asked.

"It looks that way," I said.

We were sitting in the library again, she in the green leather armchair and me on the sofa. I had made us some coffee, which she – as at her last visit – allowed to get cold. She said she was always surprised how something that smelled so good didn't taste that good, but could I bring her one anyway? She'd cut her hair, I suddenly noticed. Yesterday it had been hidden under a green scarf whose long ends hung down over her shoulders. Her new haircut made her look a little prim and proper, like a prize student. Her wild curls had been tamed – cropped short and rendered less conspicuous – however, they now revealed the beautiful shape of her head. Her mouth was very serious. Not serious in concentration like yesterday when she was taking notes – which wouldn't have been necessary since she had the dictaphone, but she had probably enjoyed acting out a scene: she the reporter and I the writer in his predictable corduroys and flannel shirt. The new look on her face today expressed suffering. I couldn't interpret it any other way, and it touched my heart. It was more than gloom or worry; something had hurt her deeply and she had come to me to talk about it. I felt my old sense of outrage. What went on down there in that apartment from which no sound was ever heard? Since Madalyn's accident almost nine years ago, I had hardly exchanged two words with Frau Reis. And to Herr Reis, I had only spoken a single time, on New Year's Day. He knocked on my door to wish me Happy New Year, which more than astonished me. He hadn't wanted to come in. He said that the year 2009 was going to be apocalyptic, and not just in an economic sense but in every possible way: meteorologically, morally, politically. A very handsome man: tall, lanky, not a trace of belly, a sharp dresser. Madalyn had her curly hair from him. While speaking to me he paced up and down in the hall, two steps in one direction, two steps back, as if he needed to go to the bathroom. For such a slim man he had a surprisingly heavy tread. I thought I caught a trace of schadenfreude in the slightly upturned corners of his mouth. I wondered how a man for whom everything on earth seemed possible could join a religious movement so hostile to life – assuming that Frau Malic's suspicions were true – a movement that turned him into an inhibited, brooding misanthrope . . . I ran into him again on the following day. He held the front door of the building open for me as I walked out to the street and then went his way with a comradely smile – but not a word of greeting – and a buoyant and not at all heavy step. Even after nine years, I was still indignant that neither he nor his wife had deemed it necessary to talk to me after Madalyn's accident. Evelyn had said to me back then that it was up to me. I was the one who intimidated people, who infected them with such a bad conscience that they would rather be impolite then run the risk of me scolding them for their irresponsibility. On the other hand, my friend Robert Lenobel –a psychiatrist and psychoanalyst after all – had taken my side. He said I should immediately begin to save money for my newly acquired problem child so she could start therapy at fourteen. The way I described her parents to him, he guessed they would have no money to spend on such a thing. – And now, in six months, Madalyn was going to turn fourteen.

She was wearing a pretty blue and white sport jacket that was probably hip. It made her look older. She leaned forward, clamped her folded hands between her knees, and looked at the floor. She had pushed up her sleeves and I saw the scar on her right forearm, a white triangle. I momentarily considered asking her about it. Maybe it would distract her from her worries if we told each other the old story we had told so often, but not for long time now.

I had the impression, however, that she didn't want to be distracted. Quite the contrary. Her breathing was labored and sometimes she held her breath and shot me a quick look, but either she didn't know how to begin, or she doubted that I was the right person to listen to her. Please, just don't confess anything to me, I thought to myself. I don't want anything to do with it. Because after having a real meeting with the real main character of the novel I was working on, I wanted nothing to do with almost anything that was taking place outside of my own head. It's a bad habit: observing other people's words, expressions, gestures, and body language and then guessing at an intention behind them that doesn't correspond to those words, expressions, and gestures but only uses them as a means to get around you. But unfortunately, it's my bad habit. I didn't want to get involved in anything else. If she wanted to tell me something, she should go ahead. But I wasn't about to ask her.

She said – and so quietly that I had to lean forward to hear her – "I can't stand my parents. I can't stand them. When I'm fifteen I'm going to take off, that's for sure. Then I'll be gone. I can't stand Mama even more than Papa. I can't stand either one of them. He's a loser. Doesn't dare say anything. He says one thing to me and another to her. It makes me want to puke."

"Please, Madalyn, I'm not interested in this," I said.

She looked at me in surprise. "You aren't? How come? I thought you couldn't stand my mother either."

"Where'd you get that idea? How can you say such a thing?"

She turned her head away, took one deep breath, hissed an apology, and ran out into the front hall.

I was really disconcerted, not least because of my smooth hypocrisy, and I ran after her. "Have you eaten anything Madalyn? Or is your mother out again? I can warm something up for the two of us. There's a risotto from day before yesterday in the refrigerator."

She rolled her eyes, climbed into her shoes, didn't bother to lace them, threw her backpack over her shoulder, and was out the door.

And yet I'd given her a clear signal I was on her side: *Or is your mother out again?* Wasn't that an unmistakable reference to her accident? Neither she nor I had said a word about her picture that hung in my library.

Chapter Three

But she returned the next day, again around noon. In the meantime, I'd flushed the risotto down the toilet. It was a leftover from an evening with Robert and Hanna Lenobel and a mutual friend. As always, I cooked too much. This time I asked Madalyn right away if she was hungry. She was. I invited her to the new restaurant in the Naschmarkt which, as advertised, was run by Samy Molcho's wife and named after her: Neni.

In my head Madalyn was still the gentle, neglected, slightly melancholy, somewhat fearful little girl, happy to play alone, who had not let go of my hand in the ambulance. Now as she sat across from me, tapping the rhythm of the music with her knuckles on the table, I was thinking that I didn't really know her. She's grown up; of course I don't know her, how would I? And I thought, no, she's not grown up. And I thought, all these years I haven't had a real picture of her. I had an image of her, but I had plucked it out of the air, from the sentimentality of my thankless heroism. She had been some preliterate thing, an inspiration for me. In fact, I had once begun to write a story that was going to have an adventure like ours at its center. But this, here, was a strain for me. I wanted to pound characters into my computer and not correct an image in reality that betrayed more about my own maudlin nature than about Madalyn. Perhaps after this day she would slip from my imagination and I was not sure that I could or would want to give her my full attention once that had happened.

We sat and waited for our order and didn't say anything. The wooden seats were made to look like old school benches. The decorator must be my age, I thought, nostalgic like me. Neni, the owner, came over to our table and shook first Madalyn's hand and then mine. I told her Madalyn's name but not what her relation was to me. Neni asked if she could treat us to a mango lassi. Madalyn nodded, but remained serious, unsmiling. One heart the mirror of another? Sheer nonsense.

"Don't you have any children?" she asked when we were alone again – a strange question.

"I have a son," I said. "His name is David. He's twenty-nine and lives in Frankfurt and works as a programmer in a computer firm. It's small but very successful and he's some kind of partner or something, but don't ask me exactly what. They develop software for people with speech impediments, if I've understood him correctly. So he does something similar to your father. In America you can earn good money doing that kind of thing and probably here too, in the future. It's a sector that's secure even in a bad economy. We talk on the telephone sometimes. But he's only visited me in Vienna once so far . . ."

None of that interested her. I was just talking away because I was afraid that if we were silent, a strange atmosphere might develop that we wouldn't be able to get out of so easily, and I would've blamed myself for that. She senses my reluctance, I thought. I'm an eccentric egoist, something I never intended to become. Her question was strange because I remembered quite clearly telling her about David, and more than once. Back then I must have represented for her an authority more than a person with the usual wagonload of possibilities. Maybe I had been an inspiration for her, as she had for me. Perhaps one heart really is the mirror of another.

"Why doesn't your wife come anymore?" she interrupted my thoughts.

"Who do you mean?"

"The woman that used to be at your house a lot. I know you're not married, but what should I call her? Once you introduced her to me. Don't you remember? Why don't you remember? We talked to each other. She was nice. And beautiful. She thought I was nice too. She had such shiny hair, like it was lacquered. How did she do that with her hair? And so black. I'm a hundred percent sure it was dyed."

I answered her questions in order, like it was an interview: that Evelyn and I had separated, that I had no idea what made her hair so shiny, and that I also knew with a hundred percent certainty that she dyed her hair.

"And now it's all over?"

"No."

"But you're not seeing each other anymore?"

"Sometimes we do. I ask her to dinner, and she says she'd rather not, and I ask her why she'd rather not, and she says because she's not hungry."

"Why do you live alone?" she continued to question me.

"I don't know," I said truthfully. "It's just the way things turned out."

"Do you like your name?"

"My first name or my last name?"

"Both."

"I've gotten used to them."

"I like my first name, but I hate my last name. When I'm eighteen, I'm going to give myself a new name. I know you can do that."

"Reis is a good name. Names of one syllable are good, easy to remember."

"I'm named after something to eat. Is that good?"

"*Reis* also means twig."

"I've never heard that before."

"*Reisig* – brushwood – I'm sure you know that. That's where *Reis* comes from. Or the other way around, *Reisig* comes from *Reis*."

"Brushwood is what you throw away when you're working in the garden, right?"

I didn't answer. Even if her name had been Gold or Diamond, at this moment she would have been sure to think of a retort.

She stirred and rearranged the wok vegetables on her plate, tasted them and added more salt, ordered a large bottle of mineral water and a Cola light, and fell to. She was famished, but in the midst of a gobble she remembered that she actually didn't want to eat anything or at least not so much. Hanna had told me that that's how it was with Clara. Clara was twenty and had recovered from a five-year struggle with bulimia – hopefully recovered.

And now at last my inner Samaritan awoke, the one who, even when I was still a child, had taken up residence near the most flammable place in my heart and my whole life long had assured me that without my help, the world and all the dear people in it would go to the dogs.

"What's up, Madalyn? What's bothering you? Tell me! What's the matter?"

Can it be that there's no one she allows to look into her heart, no one except me? And why me? Because I saved her life, which I actually didn't? I remembered one time – she must have been seven or eight – we had run into each other in front of our building one afternoon, she with her school backpack and me carrying two plastic bags full of vegetables, fruit, bread, and stuff for the weekend. We had looked at our freshly painted façade together. For weeks the building had been hung with tarps. The condo owners and the renters had voted on the color and chosen white (I had forgotten, by the way, to send in my vote on time). We had both left the building that morning when there'd been nothing to see yet, and now it was shining like a false tooth in our street. I asked her if she liked it. She said, "Not anymore." "Wait a year," I said, "then it'll get dirty and be beautiful again." Why was it so easy to see when her heart was heavy? The head of curls framed her face. She gave me a quick glance. She knit her brows and her lower lip trembled a bit. And why was her heart heavy anyway, since it was just a new paint job for the building? Hanna once told me that when Clara was a baby, she had weaned her by smearing her nipples with wormwood tea, and that ever since, her daughter had been able to conjure up that same horrified, disgusted, and insulted expression and that she, Hanna, couldn't stand to see her cry because Clara's face always reminded her of her outraged expression when, according to Hanna, "the world turned a cold shoulder on her for the first time." Since our great adventure, I had encountered Madalyn a few times crying or near to tears and there had always been an expression of absolute abandonment by the world in her face, as if the utterly bleak hopelessness of all existence had been revealed to her. "It's exactly the same building," I said. "It just looks a little bit different. Can you remember how it looked before?" "No," she said. She reached for my hand and since I was holding the heavy plastic bags and couldn't return the pressure of her hand, she took one of the two handles and pulled it out of my grasp. "I'll help you carry it," she said. She had to lift her hand to be on the same level as mine. And so we walked up the stairs to the next-to-last floor, since the elevator was blocked by scaffolding. She was about to start crying. But I didn't want to see it and had quickly continued up the last flight of stairs.

Now she looked into my eyes in a stony silence that reminded me of her mother – I'm as reckless in mistrust as in trust – and I saw it again: the tears welling up and running down her blonde lashes, her mouth screwed up, and her eyebrows trembling. She sobbed as she had sobbed during our adventure together and my hand reached for hers and without a detour through my brain it remembered what needed to be done in a situation like this. Exactly what had been done once before.

"They don't let me do anything," she blurted out. "They just won't let me do anything. Nothing at all!"

One last time an instinct warned me to stay out of this! Be an egoist. You're old enough. *You're allowed to*!

"Want to tell me about it?" I asked.

Again she looked me straight in the eye, consciously and intentionally this time as it seemed to me, even provocatively, as if she wanted to tease a spark of anger out of me that would ignite her own anger. For her fury had long since been extinguished by despair.

"I hate both of them," she said, emphasizing each word.

Chapter Four

Madalyn's German teacher Frau Petri had planned an excursion to Weimar with her ninth grade homeroom class. They were going to go during Easter vacation, leaving on Saturday and returning a week later on Easter Sunday. The popular teacher organized a trip like this every year and it was customary for her to let students from other grades take part too, especially those who were especially interested in literature or wrote especially good essays. Madalyn was one grade lower, in one of the all-girl homerooms, and she said she was the only other student Frau Petri had spoken to about this. She had waited for her after German class and said, "Madalyn, I need to talk to you. You write some of the best essays and I think you should come along. The greatest writers lived in Weimar." Madalyn had asked her parents and they had said no. Madalyn wanted to know why not, but the reason wasn't forthcoming. She said her mother told her she wouldn't give any reasons for her decisions until Madalyn was sixteen.

"Then I talked to Papa, and he said he would talk to Mama about it again. I specially asked him, As far as you're concerned, Papa, I can go? I can go as far as you're concerned? And he said, As far as I'm concerned, yes. And then he said no too. He even denied having told me the day before that he would allow me to go. He just lied! And now I can't go."

"What if your teacher talks to your mother?" I suggested.

"She already did," she answered. "But I'm sure she didn't do it right because she didn't know how important it is to me. She just called her up on the phone. If she'd really talked to her, I'm sure it would have been different. She's good at persuading people, the way she uses her hands and looks at you. It was no use. I'm not allowed."

She'd polished off all her vegetables and rice and chicken and ate a piece of New York cheesecake on top of it and was staring, blackly and overfull, at the tabletop.

"Right now it's a disappointment for you and I'm sure you're sad," I said, "but it's not a catastrophe, Madalyn."

"Oh yes it is," she said. "That's exactly what it is." There was a tiny pause and then she said without changing her tone, "Couldn't you talk to my mother?"

It had became clear to me – again, through the work on my new novel – that what I owed life was to keep my experience as much as possible to a minimum since the joy of description was incomparably greater Ever since, I had resigned myself to the life of a hermit which, if not happy, was at least comforting. I was so firmly resolved to never – never again! – get mixed up in other people's business.

"It wouldn't help," I said. "In fact, I think it would do the opposite. If your mother is wavering, which I can't imagine she is, then me interfering on your behalf would only strengthen her resolve. She can't stand me. You know that as well as I do."

"You're a famous writer. I'm absolutely sure she'd believe you."

"Believe what, Madalyn?"

"Believe how important it is for a student to go to Weimar." And now she buried her face in her hands. "It's so important to me," she said quietly. Her fingers were trembling. She rubbed her eyes and took a deep breath.

Here's what was distressing her – it shouldn't have been hard to guess: a few days ago she had met Moritz and fallen for him and she was in love was the first time in her life. He was in Frau Petri's homeroom. He was going to Weimar. And it was because of him that she wanted to go to Weimar too. Only because of him.

"If I can't go too," she said, "it's all over." She looked so sad that any argument I could think of would have been a mockery.

Actually, I couldn't think of any. I avoided looking into her small, swollen eyes. "Saturday and Sunday is already a long time," she continued, "and that's only two days, only two. I didn't see him on Saturday and Sunday because I'm not allowed out alone on Saturday and Sunday, because I'm not allowed to do anything, nothing at all, and I got grounded this Saturday and Sunday. It's so stupid, so primitive, and those were only two days and Weimar is more than a week. It's nine days all together, nine days. Please can you talk to my mother?"

She told me her love story to get me on her side – certainly that was one reason. I listened. That's my job, I told myself in justification. How many books would we abhor if we knew the story of how they had come to be? In the end, I said, "I can't do it, Madalyn, and I don't want to, either." And to fend off her dismay, and only for that reason, I added, "Why don't you ask him to stay in Vienna?"

Chapter Five

Moritz Kaltenegger was sixteen. He had had to repeat one grade and still wasn't a good student. His parents had divorced when he was ten. His mother had taken off with another man. Until recently, Moritz had lived with his father, but the two of them didn't get along. His father worked for the Viennese Municipal Insurance Company. He had little time for his son and sometimes he had a girlfriend and then it was even worse; he didn't want to leave Moritz alone during the day so he sent him to his sister's. She had two children of her own and was also divorced. On the weekends he picked Moritz up and they usually quarreled. Moritz didn't want to see his father. He couldn't stand his bad moods and knew they were only on account of him. Whenever he was at his father's house on Wolfganggasse in the twelfth district he would play basketball late into the night with the Turks in Haydn Park or get stoned out of his mind with friends on the Margaretengürtel, and finally he refused to visit his father altogether. And Herr Kaltenegger was relieved. He told his sister he couldn't control the good-for-nothing anymore. Moritz, however, got on excellently with his aunt's boyfriend. He sometimes took him fishing on the old arm of the Danube. He was an engineer and worked for companies that assembled machines. He'd been to Morocco and Tunisia and told good stories about the desert and how hot it got there.

When Moritz was not quite sixteen – fortunately for him! – he and two other guys tried to jimmy open a cigarette machine with screwdrivers and got caught. Moritz was charged with criminal damage to property and attempted robbery. In the course of pretrial mediation, he was ordered to work in an old age home after school for a certain length of time, clearing dishes and cleaning. When his time was up, the old ladies he had worked with were quite sad to see him go. He was sent to a psychologist and because the doctor smelled cigarettes on his breath, he had his things searched and they found marijuana. The child welfare office was brought in but took no further action. He was expelled from his school, however.

    His aunt's boyfriend knew the principal of the Rahlgasse Gymnasium. He described the case to her and said there were good sides to Moritz that came out if people would only be a little friendly to him. The principal accepted Moritz and put him in Frau Petri's homeroom. He liked it from the very start. He found this teacher's enthusiasm infectious, just like all her other students. Without even being asked, he wrote a poem and showed it to her. She was impressed and asked him if he would be willing to have it read and discussed in his class and also in the other classes she taught.

    Even before she knew what he looked like, even before she had said one word to him, Madalyn had heard his poem.

    Some girls in her class didn't like it. The language wasn't particularly beautiful, complained one girl who really did know quite a bit about poems and had even written some herself. Frau Petri had read her poems to the class too. Madalyn wanted to contradict the girl but couldn't think of any counter arguments. Nor would she have been able to say anything about the poem, at least not anything intelligent, except that she couldn't really concentrate on the words but even half an hour later still felt like she was hearing the poet's voice, his real voice, which she first of all had never heard before, and second of all, it had been Frau Petri who had read the poem and whose voice was totally different. How was such a thing possible? – Should she have said that out loud in class? Some of the other girls in her class would belittle her at every opportunity and treat her like she was still half a baby. They talked about things like their weight and their diets as if they were practically doctors themselves. Bea, the girl who wrote poems and had breasts that were as big as Frau Petri's and was the tallest in the class and the best student and class representative and who knows what else – she had it in for Madalyn, and just think what a field day she would've had if Madalyn had said such a thing!

But it was true! She felt like she had heard his voice through the voice of her teacher and his voice had sounded sad. Yet the poem was not a sad one. Nobody in class had thought it was. Frau Petri had even asked, "Does anyone think it's a sad poem?" Madalyn, however had been gripped by melancholy, and she looked at her feet which she always automatically placed primly together. She shoved her hands into the arms of her sweater and pulled it up over her nose so that if she started to shed some damn tears they would be absorbed right away. She felt so small, so out of it. She was envious. She was fairly certain it was envy. She knew how envy could burn and that's what this burning felt like. She felt like *she* was the one who should write a poem that would be read and discussed by the whole class. But that had never occurred to her before! She turned her notebook over and wrote on the last, blank page a few words that just popped into her head. Looking out the window didn't get her anywhere either. What did she know how to do, anyway? She knew how to make a Hungarian sweet pepper ragout. It would have been reassuring if it had been envy. But as it was, she didn't know what had upset her.

Frau Petri asked her how she liked the poem. She was startled and could only nod.

After class the girls talked about the poet. Their teacher had said he was a poet with quite a bit of talent. Everybody in the school knew what kind of guy this Moritz Kaltenegger was, namely, somebody who'd been in trouble with the police and the law, and Madalyn thought, At least I'd like to have a look at him.

During the long recess she went out to the street, folded her arms, and looked at the ground like someone lost in thought. She had the urge to press her lips against the trunk of the birch that grew next to the schoolyard gate, as she had often done in first grade when she was nervous about a test or a homework assignment – and finally, she ambled out to the flight of steps leading down to Mariahilferstrasse, her head down as if deep in thought about something deep. This was where the smokers sat. He would be one of them. She was certain she would know which one; and if she didn't recognize him by his appearance, then she surely would by his voice.

Chapter Six

Four boys were sitting on the steps of the Rahlstiege, smoking. One was standing. He had short blond hair and wore a jacket in the Red Bull colors, blue and red, with two silver stripes on the sleeves. His eyes were sunken and his mouth looked very grown-up. His mouth intimidated her. But when she was standing facing him, she didn't have to force herself at all. Everything went smoothly and on its own.

She said, "You're Moritz Kaltenegger, right?"

And he said, "How come?" It was exactly the voice that she had heard when Frau Petri was reading the poem.

"Frau Petri read your poem last period," she said. And she told him she liked it. And she asked if he had written any others.

Her mouth was brave but her heart was fearful. She could feel it hammering under her sweater and was glad that it wasn't one of her tight-fitting ones for fear he might see it. She had shoved her hands into her jeans pockets. If someone frightened her or if she felt she was being treated unfairly, it could happen that her fingers trembled. But at the same time she talked and laughed and didn't forget how words were supposed to be emphasized and glances cast, and she was pleased with the way things were going and remembered to suck in her cheeks when she listened to him so that her face looked slimmer, and everything went smoothly and on its own. How was that possible? It was as if there were two Madalyns inside her: one acted and another awarded points. She had often imagined what it would be like to fall in love. Unfortunately, she had only begun to spin the stories in her head when she had no girlfriends left. So she had no one to compare notes with. In her telephone days, when she'd had many good, close friends, such thoughts hadn't occurred to her. If you knew ahead of time you could prepare yourself. For example, point one: she would have worn something else. Today of all days she was wearing something that unfortunately had nothing special about it, her gray pullover with a high collar. She liked it because it didn't scratch and it was roomy, so for twenty hours straight she didn't have to give it a second thought – but it wasn't pretty. She had a dark red one with narrow yellow horizontal stripes. It scratched her neck and was uncomfortable but looked cool. It was the one she would have worn. Unfortunately, she didn't have a single really beautiful jacket. Her jeans were okay, no different than the other jeans that were running around.

"My class liked your poem," she said, nodding several times. "We discussed it the whole period."

"I don't like it much anymore," said Moritz Kaltenegger.

He came down the two steps and stood facing her. He was a little taller than she was and he smiled at her. Now his mouth no longer intimidated her. When he smiles, she thought, he even seems – look at him, keep looking at him! – younger than me. She thought, I bet he doesn't like his smile because it makes him look so young. But she liked it. And it was interesting how quickly he could become serious, and then his mouth looked like a man's mouth again.

He turned his back to the others. He didn't care whether they were listening or not. Was that good? Or not so good? "I wrote it a while ago," he said. "I just know it too well, if you know what I mean. At first I thought, hey! Now I don't think that anymore."

"I know just what you mean," she said. "When you've read it to yourself often enough. And then somebody else reads it, and other people talk about it."

"Exactly."

"But I think it's only like that if you wrote it yourself. Somebody else can read it five times in a row – or more – and it doesn't start to annoy them, and then when somebody else reads it out loud, it's like new again." And now she said something that wasn't true, because the untruth was praise: "Frau Petri read it twice in a row. The second time I liked it even better."

She talked and smiled and gestured with her hands and tried to get serious as quickly as he did, and at every word that was said she thought, this conversation is about to end, because soon I won't know what to say anymore. But the conversation lasted until recess was over. She said his name again, this time only his first name, and it pleased her to say it since the *Mo-* sounded like milk chocolate smells, and looked that way to, and the *–ritz* tasted sweet and hot at the same time, and if it had a color, it would be a bright red-orange.

She was proud of herself. She had had good ideas that sounded like they were from a dream, in which sometimes you don't know what something has to do with you, since you'd hardly expect something that beautiful from yourself.

They were the last two to go back inside, and when Madalyn entered her room, class had already begun.

During geography class Madalyn tried to remember every word she had said. She was oppressed by the feeling that, on balance, she had said some things that didn't please her at all now, namely, because they were so banal, so hopelessly banal. What she had found so astonishing a few minutes ago now stood there, clumsy and flat and full of contradictions. Or show-offy. Actually, nothing she had said was anything special. He would think: she's totally nothing special. And if he'd noticed the way she intentionally sucked in her cheeks when she listened to him, it would be even more embarrassing. She had clearly overdone that. But *he* was something special. That was for sure. She thought, I should've waited until tomorrow to talk to him. And before that I would have gone to Frau Petri and asked her if I could have a copy of his poem. Curiously enough, she now remembered everything *she* had said and almost nothing *he* had said. She couldn't even remember his answer when she asked if he had written other poems. He must have answered me, she thought. She did remember that he had said he had written the poem sometime or other during class. And she remembered his pale hands. They had greenish veins and looked as if they were cold. She had forgotten to tell him her name! But why hadn't he asked her? He didn't even know her name – what was the point of the bees buzzing in her head if he didn't even know her name!

Geography was one of her favorite subjects. Not because she was interested in countries and capitals and poverty and burned-down rain forests, but because – and she didn't have the least idea why it was so – there was no other subject where she could drift off so wonderfully. If there was a subject that was fit for writing poems in, then it was geography. Maybe it was because of the names of cities and rivers and countries and presidents that she got confused and couldn't remember and didn't even try to remember because Herr Lunzer only gave good grades anyway. It was so funny: when something meant something to her, afterwards she couldn't remember what it was, but only what she had felt about it, and the more important something was to her, the less she could remember it. Maybe somebody could explain that to her sometime! She really couldn't remember a single word of his poem. She turned her geography notebook over and wrote down a sentence and then another and then another. Was that already a poem? When did you know? She would never show such a thing to anyone. If he asked her what she liked best about his poem she would not be able to tell him. Her heart jumped into her throat: maybe he *had* asked her. And what had she replied? Maybe he had done nothing but ask her questions and she had just babbled away and not answered any of them. Because she wasn't listening. She could only listen if something didn't interest her too much.

She was sitting at one of the tables along the side. Bea Haintz was sitting up front. In German and geography Bea sat at the front, in the other classes she sat in the back. And the others put up with that and were even willing to trade seats with her. To get a plus from Bea was something special. Because Bea was something special. When she sat in front, she displayed her complacent profile to the class. And now that complacent profile was saying, I criticized him but I'm the only one that understands. And I don't, thought Madalyn. The objections Bea had raised to the poem had wounded her as if they were aimed at her. It wouldn't have been at all hard to say the following sentence to him: *I'd like to talk to you some more about your poem.* It was probable that in that case they would have agreed to meet after school. Maybe he lived in her direction? They could have walked partway together. Why on earth hadn't she said that? Instead of saying all that junk! She hoped so hard she'd see him on the street after school. Then she could make up for her mistakes. What would he think if she said to him, I don't remember your poem but I thought it was really beautiful because I could hear your voice? For example, she could say that it had felt like music. It sounded so beautiful and that's why she couldn't pay attention to the contents. Yes, that's exactly what she'd say. I got carried away by your poem. Frau Petri had said the more things a poem sets free in the listener, the better it is. Some poems were like music and some were able to carry you away. She'd probably said the same thing to her homeroom class. When Frau Petri made a longer pause after saying something, it meant she was giving you time to take notes. And she didn't call it a binder, she said notebook. So it wouldn't be a disaster to admit to him that she didn't remember his poem, because it had "freed up so much in me." However, she wasn't completely comfortable with this strategy.

Either he had already left or he was still inside, in his classroom. She recognized one of the four boys who had been sitting on the steps with him, smoking. She assumed he was in Moritz Kaltenegger's homeroom. Should she ask him? Is Moritz still up in your room? Did Moritz go home already? Where's Moritz? She didn't dare. She waited in front of the school, walked in circles, again had the urge to kiss the birch tree, and waited until she was alone. Finally she went up to his homeroom.

The room was empty. Which desk was his? She sat down at the one that was farthest from the teacher's desk. There was a biology book on the shelf under the desktop. But there was no name in it. She reached farther back on the shelf and pulled out a crumpled candy bar wrapper. That was all. Just a Milka Nut. She sniffed at the book. It smelled like smoke. That didn't necessarily mean anything. She closed her eyes, pressed the book against her forehead. But what did she think was going to happen? That she would hear his voice in her head again: Yes, it's mine?

She walked her bicycle home. Gave herself time because she had time and the way home seemed to her like a movie.

Chapter Seven

Madalyn's parents didn't own many books and they had no poetry at all. Now and then they went to concerts at the Musikverein and on All Saints Day they heard Mozart's Requiem in St. Stephen's Cathedral; they had also once been invited to an opera when some Chinese partners of the firm Madalyn's father worked for were in town. Her mother loved musicals but said there hadn't been one worth going to in Vienna in a long time. She had just finished making ground beef and noodles when Madalyn got home. Madalyn set the table for two, carefully placing the spoon and fork to the right of each plate on top of the napkin folded into a triangle, and at the top of each plate a glass for mineral water. Her mother had always put a cushion on Madalyn's chair and couldn't get out of the habit – or didn't want to.

Madalyn said that in German class they were reading poems at the moment. Everyone was supposed to bring a poem to class and they were the only ones who had no poetry at home. Her mother knew one by heart. She couldn't remember who the author was and also didn't know if the poem was good or kind of lame. Besides, she only knew the first verse:

I built the house myself
from the cellar to the roof.
How is it that a goblin
lives underneath the stairs?

They laughed at the human brain – that funny, giant walnut – still being able to reel off such a funny poem after thirty years, but it couldn't retain an important telephone number because you could store those in your cell phone.

"And that's how come," said her mother, while running her hand through Madalyn's short hair and scratching her scalp with her fingernails, "I can see a number on the screen three times a day and still can't remember it."

In those days, Madalyn was getting along pretty well with her mother; there were still two weeks to go before she would ask if she could go to Weimar, the "City of the Classics," with Frau Petri's class. Nevertheless, Madalyn was cautious. Talking on the telephone was a touchy subject.

Madalyn made the salad. She could do it quick as a flash and her salads were better than her mother's. Which Frau Reis was happy to admit. Madalyn often bought the ingredients herself and added surprises like chopped nuts scattered into the salad, or toasted croutons or roasted pumpkin seeds. For a while she had a lot of fun with salads, downloading recipes from the internet. High point: a Waldorf salad. Her father called them "Madalyn's famous salads." Currently, she was restricting herself to ordinary green salads with tomatoes and cucumbers. She experimented with the dressing, but only because none of her dressings really tasted good to her. The vinegar was too sour and she'd always found the oil a little icky. A lemon, sour cream, and dill dressing she had seen on the internet had too many calories and too much bad fat. She preferred to eat salad without any dressing and even without salt and pepper. On the other hand, then all she had to do was to wash and cut the vegetables and that was certainly no skill she could take credit for.

For a quarter of an hour she had forgotten her "dreamy swirl," but now it was back again. She wrote the words hastily on the edge of the newspaper, tore the piece off, and put it in her pocket. It might fit into a poem. The thought made her happy.

After lunch she tried on the red and yellow pullover in her room. She wasn't completely sure about it anymore. When she looked at herself straight on in the big mirror in her parents' bedroom, she didn't think she looked so phenomenal, not at all.

She knew everything about the person facing her. Did the same thing happen to Moritz Kaltenegger? What about when he looked at his mouth in the mirror? He must know that he had an interesting mouth. When she walked past the mirror and pretended to accidentally catch sight of herself, it was better. She played a very busy woman, stressed out, took three quick steps and made a face as if she was saying, I'd have to look at that in more detail. And then she walked deliberately, moving her mouth and hands as one did when deep in a profound and perhaps even melancholy conversation. Or she stuck her hands in her back pockets and lifted her head: a young woman who had just thought of the first line of a poem – that pleased her the most. It was also good when she laughed: an animated person at a party. She laughed without making a sound. Did she have a pretty laugh? Or a dull, ordinary laugh? She thought her laugh was rather nice. Once a couple had been guests in their home, friends of her parents – or not really friends, otherwise they would have come more often. At any rate, the woman had a laugh that stuck in Madalyn's memory. When she laughed she had tilted her head to the side and looked at the ground and somehow directed her laugh with her hand. Madalyn tried it out in front of the mirror. Looked good when she did it, too. She was going to start laughing that way in class the very next day. Just don't overdo it again! Would she talk to him again in the long recess? She didn't want to be pushy, but she also didn't want to just stand there and wait for him to come to her. She was afraid of being hurt. Perhaps she would just stay in the classroom during the long recess. What then? That would also be just waiting, a worse kind of waiting. Maybe she should just stay home tomorrow. And wait. But at home, a much worse kind of waiting. She would have liked to see herself from behind. Or from above. How did she look from behind when she was walking? Most people see you from behind. Especially when you have a particular expression on your face. Then people turn around after they pass you. And they look at you longer and more intently from behind then from the front. He had a laid-back way of turning his torso when he spoke. What about when someone's looking out the window and I'm going past down below, she thought. What would that person think? Who was there she could ask? She didn't have a girlfriend who would be honest with her. The way she walked was pretty certainly not fantastic. She had bad posture. At least, that's what her mother said. But she was capable of saying so on purpose just to needle her. It was very probable that exactly what her mother called bad posture was laid-back. What her mother called good posture was something Madalyn pretty certainly didn't want.

"It's probably a mistake for us not to have more books," said her mother while they were putting their dishes into the dishwasher. "It's something you have to start doing early on."

"It doesn't matter," said Madalyn.

She had a ten euro bill and seventy cents left over from her allowance. She was saving, but she didn't know what for. She called to her mother that she was going out briefly to buy something. She left on the red and yellow sweater. She didn't put on her jacket. Although it was too cold for what she had on, it was less than a hundred yards to Anna Jeller's bookstore on Margaretenstrasse. When she passed a store window she would look to see how she looked in it. It must be heavenly, she thought, to see a photo somewhere with a really pretty girl on it and have it turn out to be yourself.

Frau Jeller was standing in front of her shop smoking a cigarette. She said Madalyn should go on in and have a look around. She'd be right there.

Madalyn was the only customer. The cast iron stove against the back wall was going. There was a nice smell of coffee and old books. The bookshelves reached to the ceiling. A library ladder was leaning against the wall next to the stove, its treads covered with velvet or suede. There were leather armchairs in the corners, a red one and a yellow one, with oval side tables next to them covered with coffee cups, a sugar bowl, a plate of cookies, and wine glasses. She had heard that starting with the ninth grade, Frau Petri would ask each of her students after every vacation – summer, Christmas, between terms, and Easter – what they had read in their free time. There was a contest to see who could name the most interesting book, a book that Frau Petri would describe as the most interesting. Every time, they would search the internet for summaries of content and interpretations, and if you were lucky – or unlucky – Frau Petri would ask you to prepare a little report about the book for the next class. Madalyn pictured herself standing in front of the class and talking about an important novel or play – you were also allowed to name a play, even if you hadn't read it but only seen it. Madalyn had never been to the theater, nor did she have any desire to go. She had also never thought about being an actress, not even a movie star. They probably wouldn't want someone with such curly hair anyway. She didn't care. Once Frau Petri had said that you could have different opinions about reading, but really there was only one reason for anyone to read a book, namely, because they were looking for a story that told about what they had already experienced, and because they wanted to know how someone else would behave in a similar situation. It could be, thought Madalyn, that among all these books there was one that told about a girl who was like her and to whom something similar was happening, a book that in fact told how her story was going to continue. She would buy that book – no, she would come to this bookstore every day and always read a little bit ahead in her life, one day ahead, not more, only one day. How would the book end? Suddenly she felt a warm wave rising within her. It felt so good here, and Frau Jeller standing out on the sidewalk smoking a cigarette seemed to be like a friend. She could well imagine that she would soon become someone who browsed here and asked questions and talked about her own ideas. She really thought it had never been so good to be alive.

Nobody in her class was really interested in books. Everybody admired Frau Petri and loved being in her class, but nobody spent money on books. Not even Bea Haintz. Here's how it was with Bea: when she saw women running the hundred-yard dash on TV, she seemed to herself to be the best hundred-yard sprinter. When the news reported that Gerline Kaltenbrunner was planning to climb every mountain over 26,000 feet, she pretended she would do the same thing in a few years. And she gossiped about Brad Pitt and Angelina Jolie as if she visited them every Christmas. And after Frau Dr. Rachinger, the director of the Austrian National Library, came to their school to talk about her work, Bea acted like she was already her designated successor. Madalyn vowed never to tell anyone about this bookstore. She wanted it for herself. Or for herself and someone else. Because sometimes they would come here together, but not very often. She would leaf through a book of poems and say to Moritz Kaltenegger, Here, read this! It would be a passage that had to do with them, except that no one else would ever guess that. And he would show her a passage, and it would be the same one. But she would understand a little more about poems than he did. He could write beautiful poems, but she would understand them better. That would be possible. Why not? She thought she was probably not the kind of person who wrote poems.

There were little piles of the newest books displayed on a long table in the middle of the store. Madalyn ran her hand over them. What there was to be read in them ascended into her hand and up her arm into her armpit and she thought, there isn't a store in the whole city that I love as much as this one. But this was the first time she was here and she had never bought a book in her life. And what if Bea had been waiting for Moritz Kaltenegger after school? And they had walked together for a while? And what if she had talked to him about his poem? And had made a date with him? Then Madalyn would have no chance.

Madalyn could hardly pull herself together when Frau Jeller walked up to her.

She said – and had to start again because she had a frog in her throat – that she needed a book of poems but, she added and shrugged her shoulders, it couldn't cost more than €10.70 because that was all the money she had.

"What kind of poems are you interested in?" asked Frau Jeller and smiled. Now she clearly had a beautiful smile. "Classic poems or more modern ones?"

Madalyn didn't know exactly what classic poems were; she hastily replied in the kind of voice you would use if you were not there for yourself but in some official capacity, "Love poems, modern ones." And then she laughed and tilted her head to the side and looked at the ground. She didn't trust herself to conduct her laugh with her hands, because she hadn't practiced that in front of the mirror yet.

"Do you know the name of a writer you're interested in? Or would you like a volume with poems by various writers?"

"Yes, that, various ones."

Frau Jeller took a small hardbound volume from the shelf. "This costs €10.30, and it's all love poems by modern writers."

The book had a dust jacket in pale white, pink, and yellow and bore the title *No Promises* and the subtitle *Contemporary Love Poems*.

Without opening it, Madalyn bought it and left. She was a little embarrassed and didn't know why, like she had somehow gotten the book under false pretenses.

Chapter Eight

Her cell phone's display showed eight new calls.

Her mother had left already. There was a piece of paper on the kitchen table with poem about the goblin under the stairs written out in a clear hand. "See you at six, Madi."

Eight new calls.

Her prepaid card had run out, two weeks ago already. Madalyn's goal was to get by for a month with a ten-euro card and even have a tiny bit left over. Since January she had succeeded, that is, in January and February she had. But she failed in March. She had run out of minutes by the middle of the month. It was a drag. When her minutes were used up she could receive calls, but not send any. She hardly got called anymore on account of the fact that she herself could telephone only seldom and briefly. This had come about because she was trying to be a better person. When she came home from school she looked to see if anybody had dialed her number or sent a text message. Sometimes she didn't look until the evening. And she realized proudly but also sadly that there were even times when she hadn't thought about phoning all day long. For a while she'd kept a telephone diary, as a check. By now she didn't need that anymore. She hoped she didn't. The little book had three columns per page. In one she was supposed to enter who had called her and when, in the second whom she had called and when and how long she had talked, and in the third what the conversation was about. Whenever she saw the dark blue notebook in her desk drawer, she got an creepy feeling, as if evil spirits might fly out if she opened it. The notebook had been her father's idea. "It can be your telephone diary," he said when he gave it to her, putting his hands on hers. "It will be your friend." No, it never became her friend. She was nine when she started to use a cell phone. She was often alone and her parents had bought her a dull greenish Nokia with rounded corners. She got bored in the afternoons and she phoned her classmates. They all had cell phones, but they were from different carriers – T-Mobile, A1, Orange, Bob, Telering – and that drove up the costs. When she was alone, it wasn't long before she couldn't let five minutes go by without tapping on the little keys. She phoned while doing her homework or heating up her lunch, she phoned in front of the TV, and she even kept her cellphone with her when she went to the bathroom. It was always in her hand or lying right next to her hand. And then one day there had been a horrible row. She couldn't remember anymore how high the charges had been, only that in a single month she had sent more than a thousand text messages. Her mother gave her holy hell and her father just kept saying "You're sick Madalyn, you're sick" over and over again.So she had firmly resolved to be a better person. Her mother canceled her cell phone plan. If Madalyn wanted to make a call, she told her, she'd have to buy a phone card with her allowance money. At night, she dreamed about telephoning: keys, beeps, texting thumbs and so on. It had been a hard time for her. She ran through her first phone card in one afternoon. After three days, her allowance was used up. She blundered around the apartment like an animal in the zoo, her phone in her hand, and when the redemptive ring tone (the beginning of a pop song) finally sounded, she was pressing the green button before it even stopped ringing. Not being able to make calls was like being in prison.

And now eight new calls were waiting for her! All from the same number!

And only then did she think of what should have occurred to her immediately: it must be him. But what if it wasn't? What if somebody was trying to make fun of her? She had the urge to lock herself in the bathroom and lie in a tub full of hot water, where even a condemned murderer would be left in peace for half an hour. She felt like someone was trying to expose her to the ridicule of the entire class. Perhaps at that very moment they were all sitting together and giggling, everyone looking at their cell phones and waiting for her to call back so they could laugh themselves silly. She sat down on the kitchen floor with her legs outstretched and put her cell phone down in front of her. The little device was making her unhappy.

Eight new calls and all within the last half hour. Right when she had been in the bookstore.

Whoever had tried to call her eight times in thirty minutes – and nothing was certain, absolutely nothing – would surely try a ninth time. She divided thirty by eight. So, on average every three and a half minutes he – or she – had called. But probably he. She waited. After five minutes, she couldn't stand it anymore. Her stomach was tied in knots. When she stood up she was dizzy. When she thought about spaghetti with tomato sauce she thought she'd have to throw up. She drank a big glass of water in a single gulp. It was not at all a sure thing that Moritz Kaltenegger had called her! How would he get her number? He didn't even know her name.

She searched the kitchen for money. Sometimes there was change lying around. In a cup in the cupboard she found a two-euro coin and three twenty-cent pieces. Why did she have to buy that book! She hadn't even looked at it. She opened it, skimmed a poem, and it was meaningless. What kind of love poem was that supposed to be? She had memorized every word. She could have said the poem by heart. Why on earth had she bought this book! €10.30! As much as the cheapest telephone card cost! Nobody in her class had a book of poems of their own. Not even Bea Haintz. She rifled through the pockets of the coats hanging in the closet. She found fifty cents in her father's winter coat. Along with what remained of her allowance, that made €3.50. She didn't know anyone who would loan her €6.50. She rifled through the drawers in the living room, the drawers of her parents' night tables, and searched the closet again. She crawled around on the floor looking under the furniture and lifted up the laundry basket in the bathroom. There was so little furniture in the apartment, there was hardly any opportunity to hide things, and no hope of finding anything.

She went into the bathroom and ran water into the tub and then let it run out again. She kept her cell phone in her hand – like before, when she'd been sick. He wouldn't call again. No normal person calls up eight times in half an hour. He had called up eight times. Nobody could expect him to call a ninth time. She put her hand between the cushions in the living room, picked up the corners of the rug, and looked again into the cups in the kitchen cupboard.

At last, she set off for the bookstore with her poems. And Frau Jeller was nice enough to take the volume back and return her money. She even followed Madalyn out to the street and said the same thing sometimes happened to her – although there was no way she could know what had happened to Madalyn – and she hoped she would stop by again. "We could talk about poems. I like poems too, very much in fact," she said.

Madalyn felt like no sooner had she gained this cozy, cheerful place of happiness than she had to lose it again. She ran to the Kettenbrückengasse subway station on the Wienzeile, bought a telephone card in the kiosk, and entered the code on her cell phone. She didn't want to telephone on the street. It was too loud. She didn't want to do it at home either. She ran to the little park where she had learned how to ride her bike.

A mother and two children were sitting on a bench. Madalyn withdrew to the farthest corner of the park. It took a while for her breathing to calm down. And finally she pressed the button to call the number that had tried to reach her eight times.

Moritz Kaltenegger said, "Hello, Madalyn."

She said, "Hello, Moritz."

Chapter Nine

They ended up agreeing to meet in front of the Urania movie theater; it was halfway between them. Moritz's aunt lived in the second district, near the Prater. Out of caution and consideration and embarrassment, they had a complicated time agreeing on a meeting place. Every time he said her name on the telephone, his voice jumped into the upper register, and it was no different when she said his; sometimes she exaggerated it so that she would sound like him. He also talked about his aunt and his aunt's boyfriend and what it was like living with them. Madalyn didn't dare ask if he'd like to see her and she longed for him to say something that would let her know he was talking about the two of them, only about the two of them. Because then she would have said it was hard to talk about it on the telephone, and he might have said he wanted to see her. They talked about school and the other students and the teachers, which really didn't interest her and surely didn't interest him either. He certainly hadn't called her up eight times for that – eight times in half an hour! And suddenly, everything had been said and there was silence. She could hear him breathing like is when you hold your hand over the receiver. In her excitement, she couldn't find a single useful thought and couldn't recall anything they had talked about during recess that she could now pick up and spin out.

So she sat there with the diabolical little instrument at her ear that had brought her so much misfortune and trouble and now, perhaps, happiness.

He started to talk again.

He was so glad she had come over and started talking to him, he said. He never would have dared to do it himself. She said she didn't believe him. He couldn't have even been aware she existed. He said she was wrong, really wrong about that. In the background she heard an ambulance go by. Was he outside on the street? Why was he on the street? Was it impossible for him to phone her from where he lived? Or was he on his way somewhere, going to meet the tough kids who were his friends? That would be a shame, she thought. Then he has no time for me. He said that he'd tried to reach her a couple times already. But he didn't say how he knew her name and her telephone number. That could remain his secret, she thought. She pictured him lying in her arms and saw how she cradled him, how she said his name over and over, and how she whispered that he could cry if he wanted to, for she had no doubt that he did want to and that she was the only person who knew that, and the only one he didn't need to feel ashamed around. They didn't say a word about poetry. He shouldn't think she was only interested in his poem. It was *also* about his poem but not *only* about it. Would it be better for him to think she was interested in him because she liked his poem or that she liked his poem because she was interested in him?

"I'd like to see you," she said at last, closing her eyes and holding her breath and pressing her fingernails into her thumb, thinking the marks would still be there tonight. And what then? She said something and added his name and her heart sent out tiny prickles in every direction; she could feel them in her hands, a pain she wanted to have always and yet never again: to hear his name, even said by her own voice; to just hear him and not see him. As if she had really seen him at least once already. But I haven't, she thought, haven't *really* seen him, and her thoughts were uncomfortable because she really couldn't explain anything to herself anymore. I wish I hadn't said it, she thought. She wished she could take a break, that both of them would hang up and resume the conversation in a quarter of an hour.

They could walk along the Danube Canal, he said. He'd like to show her something.

"What?" she asked.

"I'm not gonna tell you."

Madalyn hugged herself, laid her head on her shoulder, and held the cell phone between her shoulder and her ear. She couldn't remember exactly what he looked like. How could she have forgotten! She wasn't even a hundred percent sure about his mouth. The whole time, she had an urge to imitate the sound of his voice – it was a habit of hers, imitating voices, a talent that had often earned her applause. He might think she was making fun of him. Good thing I thought of that in time, she told herself; she'd better be careful. Sometimes her imitations happened automatically and precisely when someone was important to her.

"Shall we meet right now?" he asked.

"I'll take the subway," she said.

"I'll ride my bike," he said.

"I could come by bike too."

"Which will it be?"

"I guess I'll take the subway."

"So we'll hang up and go?"

"Hang up and go," she said.

"Hang up and go."

She saw him before he saw her. His bicycle was leaning against the wall of the theater and he was standing beside it, one hand on the handlebars and the other on the saddle. His legs were crossed. He had a cigarette between his lips and it was angled steeply up. The smoke was getting in his eyes and he was squinting. His hair was wet and unkempt. Madalyn told herself she would ask him where he'd bought such a cool jacket; she'd like to have one herself. The next time there was a silence between them (not the beautiful silence she had been imagining during the ride over here, a silence she would have no trouble maintaining, but a mute, dangerous nothing that swallowed every thought that came into your head), she would come out with her question about his jacket to build a bridge over that nothingness, and then follow up by asking, Had he, like, bought the jacket because it had the same colors as Red Bull? If he answered he didn't care about that, she would say she didn't either, it had just occurred to her. However, it would be better not even to start talking about that. But she wanted to be prepared with at least *one* topic in case they both got stuck. She couldn't concentrate on a single thought. She had nothing left inside of her.

When he caught sight of her, he quickly took the cigarette out of his mouth and threw it on the ground. He came over to her and gave her his hand. Nobody else would do that, she thought. As she had expected his hand, a large hand, was cold.

"Hello Madalyn," he said again.

"How do you know my name?" she finally asked.

He smiled and shrugged. She liked him a lot, and again, especially his mouth.

"Nobody else has a name like yours," he said. "It's a great name. Everybody knows your name, everybody in our class. It's easy to forget a name if a lot of people have it, because it's easy to get it mixed up with some other name a lot of people have. If somebody is named Meier, you ask yourself, Was his name Meier or Müller? You forget it more easily than when somebody has a complicated name, where you don't know right away exactly how to say it."

"You think so?"

"I do think so. Definitely."

She wasn't sure he really meant it. Or if he was teasing her. But she wouldn't get angry at him because of that. "Moritz isn't all that common either," she said.

"More common than Madalyn anyway. I guarantee there's no one in the whole school who knows another Madalyn. I think you're the only Madalyn in Vienna."

The thought startled her. And she was also startled to see how nervous he was. He doesn't need to be, she thought. When she was very nervous, she tended to give up, withdraw, just run away; because she was afraid she couldn't take it anymore. She had been known to play hooky from tests and invent excuses just because she was so nervous; one time she had pretended to faint in class before a test and had convinced everybody, too. The idea of beginning a new life at once, under a different name, in another country, another continent – Africa for example – without parents, with just a little English, would restore a bit of her equanimity in such situations. These scenarios always ended with her dying, but that didn't scare her. She didn't know why, but she thought that Moritz was like her. She was convinced of it, convinced that he thought the same, felt the same, liked the same movies and spaghetti with straight tomato sauce, so that it wouldn't have surprised her if he had turned around, gotten on his bike, and ridden away. Except that he would really emigrate and not just imagine doing it. Everything she knew about him convinced her of that.

There was a bicycle path behind the Urania that ran along the embankment and in a long curve down to the Danube Canal. He asked if she thought she'd be able to ride on the bike with him. She'd just have to sit on the crossbar because his rear luggage carrier was rusted out.

He held the bike steady while she got on, grasped the handlebars and braced her feet on the frame. At first he pushed her along like that, then he took a running start and jumped on the saddle and immediately started pedaling hard. They rode downhill and got going really fast.

"How do you like this?" he shouted. "Do you like it? I think it's fantastic!"

She actually wanted to scream. She was afraid and felt sick to her stomach. His chest was touching her shoulder. She leaned forward, confused by his sudden proximity, and he was more of a stranger than ever before. She had an urge to jump off and run away. She heard his breath at her ear and leaned even farther forward over the handlebars. A man and a woman were walking toward them and they jumped aside. Madalyn caught a glimpse of a bright face and a friendly smile.

"I'd like to get off when we get to the bottom," she said.

"I just wanted to do this one stretch cause you can get going so fast," he said.

He braked, got off the bike, and held it steady.

Madalyn stayed on the crossbar. Now everything was okay. Now she liked it that his hands were right next to hers on the handlebars and the entire width of his chest was touching her side. He smelled of cigarette smoke. She thought it was a pleasant smell.

"Why did you get your hair cut short?" he asked. Now he was walking the bike, going very slowly, and since it was downhill he squeezed the brakes repeatedly.

"How do you know about that?" she asked.

"Your hair was like your name," he said. "You're the only one with hair like that."

"Like what?"

"Like what you used to have."

"Like what?" she asked again.

"Like, big hair."

"Yeah, pretty big, unfortunately."

"I don't know anybody with so many curls on their head."

"They're mostly gone now."

"They'll grow back," he said.

"It looks better this way," she said. She wasn't worried that he wouldn't like the way her hair was now. It was curly in any case, with smaller curls, and she looked older. It definitely looked prettier shorter. Everybody in her class said so. Her new haircut had been *the* event of the day. In the meantime, another girl had also gotten her hair cut short; although she would say it had nothing to do with Madalyn, it was enough that the others thought so. There was no question but that they listened to the Madalyn with short hair more than they had listened to the Madalyn with a big head of curls. The proof was her father: when he came home that evening, he hadn't recognized her at first. He even admitted it. And he somehow acted different, more friendly in any case, courteous, as if there was something exotic about her that made him uneasy and more respectful. After she had thoroughly examined herself in the mirror and tried out how she looked in a dozen poses, moods, and snapshots, she realized that with a head of curls she had always looked like a child: cute, stubborn, droll. And then that leads to walking like a child and using your hands like a child and finally talking like a child – sometimes she could have bit her tongue. Now when she happened to see herself in a shop window, it seemed that everything about her was different. After only a few days, everything about her was different, better.

Moritz stopped pushing, and she got off the bike.

"Was that what you wanted to show me?" she asked.

He shook his head and displayed the grin in which his teeth became visible in one corner of his mouth.

"You want a cigarette too?" he asked.

"No," she said.

"Haven't you ever smoked?"

"No."

"I want to break the habit, anyway," he said and put his cigarette back in the pack.

Chapter Ten

The surprise was graffiti Moritz had sprayed onto a wall on the other side of the Danube Canal just a few days before. It covered an entire section of the wall, fifteen feet high and twenty feet wide, and consisted mostly of the four letters L, E, S, and S—in brilliant white surrounded by black shadows—which formed the upper part of the graffiti. The background was light blue and beneath the letters it said "is novb" or "is movd" or "is morb," Madalyn couldn't really make it out.

"I'm Less," said Moritz. "That's my nickname. How do you like it?"

Next to his picture was another one of a comic-book witch, poisonous green and wearing a black dress. She was riding a broomstick past skyscrapers that each had a face – surprised, angry, stupid, and sad.

"Weird," said Madalyn, "like, weird somehow." But she was talking more about the witch than the four gigantic letters stretching all the way up the wall to the sidewalk above, as if they had oozed out of the asphalt and congealed or had been clamped under the road surface so they wouldn't fall down. Exacty, that's just what he intended, she thought, now I see. And the black around the letters wasn't a shadow, it was a side view, so the letters looked like giant blocks jutting out from the wall. But they only became blocks further down. Toward the top the black part got thinner and folds had also been sprayed on, so that it looked like the block letters had been squashed together up there. Now I get it, she thought.

"How did you do that?" she asked. "It's incredibly high. Did you paint it from above or below?"

"All from below, with a ladder. It'd be too dangerous from above and you'd have to think upside down. I found a couple of wooden ladders somewhere and a third one that was shorter and I fastened them together with duct tape."

"Did anyone help you?"

"Not a soul. And I did it all at night, when you can't hardly see anything. I hung the ladders on my bike and two big grocery bags full of spray cans. You wouldn't believe how many cans you need for such a big area. And you have to wear a face mask because the stuff is poisonous. And if somebody comes by in the dark and sees you with the mask on, they think you're a terrorist and they're gonna call the police on their cell and the cops'll put a gun to your head, thanks a lot. It's a lot of stress. Usually you don't do it alone, you always bring someone along as a lookout. I did it at one go and all alone, without stopping, from two a.m. to four a.m. But I made an exact sketch beforehand. It was so cool to do it, and I really liked it. It's the biggest one I've done so far. At first I rode here three times a day to look at it. I could've sat here for hours just looking at it, it's such a great feeling. But now it's not such a big deal anymore. Because usually graffiti like this only lasts a day or two or three before somebody else sprays over it."

"But that's so mean!"

"No, no. That's how it is. I do it too, it's the way it is. If somebody comes along and thinks they've got something better, they spray over yours. That's what I do too. But you don't dare do it to the really good ones, or you just don't want to because you like them and you want them to stay there."

"I like it a lot," said Madalyn.

"Actually, it's not allowed over there," he said. "You're actually not allowed to spray there. You can do it on this side, but it's not as good. The trees are in front of it, for one thing. If they catch you spraying over there, you have to pay a fine. But they've never caught me."

"It's a real work of art," she said.

"Yeah, it really is," he said.

He had parked his bike. They stood side by side, their upper arms brushing against each other. They looked over at the other side of the Danube Canal, and now there was the silence between them that Madalyn had feared. She sensed that Moritz was trying to say something. "Yeah" he said and "Exactly." But that was like saying nothing at all. Either nothing occurred to him or he was uncertain if he really wanted to say what he wanted to say.

He took hold of her hand and everything was good.

"You can paint and write poems," she said, happy that she didn't have to pretend anymore. "That's great, it's really great."

And then he told her how it was with the poem. How it really was, that is. He said he hadn't written it. The L and E and S and S shone across to them like letters on the testimony of an eyewitness. Moritz giggled. He giggled in a high voice with more air than tone. He said Frau Petri had been talking about poetry. For the whole period she had talked about nothing but poems and songs, and that songs were also poems and that she thought more poems were being written in the world today than ever before. She suggested that everybody in the class should look for a poem. The internet was full of poems and you could find one and print it out and put it into your pocket and pull it out and read it anytime – in the subway, or waiting in line at the supermarket, or when the movie on TV was interrupted for commercials. She passed out sheets with a list of internet addresses and said she once did that for a whole year— carried a new poem in her pocket each week—and it had been wonderful. After class, everybody ran to the media room and started looking on the net. He, Moritz, had not done so. He sat down that night at his aunt's computer and after two hours of looking, he finally found a poem he sort of liked. But then his aunt's printer had been fucked up so he copied out the poem by hand. The next German class, everybody pulled out their poems, all in printouts, and only his was handwritten. Since he hadn't been in homeroom 9B very long, he usually held back pretty much. And besides, his handwriting was shitty and everybody didn't need to see it, so he went up to Petri after class and showed her his poem and asked what she thought of it. Somehow she must have misunderstood what he was saying. She read the poem and said she was impressed. She even congratulated him. And he thought, aha, I made a good choice. He hadn't taken the easy way out. He'd read at least twenty poems, surfed from one website to another, and finally decided on this poem. Frau Petri said it was every bit as good as the poems that kids had downloaded from the internet. But he'd been slow on the uptake. It hadn't occurred to him that she might think he'd written the poem himself. Never in his life had he had the urge to write a poem. Why would he? But that's exactly what she thought, and only because his was the only poem written by hand. At some point he did realize there had been a misunderstanding, but by that time it was too late.

"I think," he said, "I mean, she would have looked kind of dumb. She would have, not me. Maybe I would too, but not as dumb as her. I didn't mean for it to happen. See, Madalyn? She got so carried away. She read the poem back to me, out loud, and by then other people were already standing around listening."

He leaned into her arm, took hold of her shoulder, turned her toward him, and looked into her eyes, and she returned his gaze and was not frightened by what he had just told her.

"I made that picture over there," he said, "but not the poem. Sorry, Madalyn. She exaggerated so much. I wanted to say something the whole time. And at some point, it was too late. It would have been like I was shitting everybody, see? She just wanted me to have written something. But I didn't write it. And everybody was gaping at me. You're the only one that knows," he said and let go of her.

She had never once thought about poems until today. To her, poems were just like anything else. It was okay with her that Moritz Kaltenegger was not a poet. But the fact that she was the only person in the world he had told – that was beautiful.

"It doesn't matter," she said.

"But I did make the picture," he said.

"It's really interesting," she said.

"I come here every day and think, maybe I should have made something else, but then I think, there was nothing else I should've made."

"It's a really beautiful picture," said Madalyn. She forgot to ask what the letters under the big LESS meant.

Chapter Eleven

Moritz wanted to walk her home but she didn't want him to. He shook her hand as he had when they met, got onto his bike, and rode off. Madalyn didn't watch him go. When she did turn around to look he had disappeared.

She put her hands in her pockets, lifted her head, and knew that she looked like her image in the mirror at home when she had played a happy young woman. She was glad to be alone. It was too much all at once, and if there had been even more, one thing might have gotten mixed up with another. There was more springtime down here near the water and the trees than up above in the city, but even the dust smelled of spring. She folded her arms and walked in aimless circles, recalling every detail, beginning with the moment she had seen him standing in front of the Urania wearing jeans with ragged bottoms. She thought she could read his mind, what he'd been thinking at that moment; it was easy for her to sort it out. She could understand him better than herself, and she thought she was a little bit more interesting than he was. He knows himself, she thought. However, that could mean that he hasn't been as bowled over as me. When it hits you, you don't know what to do. On the other hand, he talked too much, and that's what you do when you don't know what to do. But what was going to come of this? It didn't necessarily at all mean that he had fallen in love with her. And I said almost nothing, she thought. She thought she already knew one of his peculiarities, even after such a short time: when he talked for a longer stretch, he looked you briefly in the eye, put his head to one side, stared at the ground, and only lifted his eyes again at the end. Her father had the habit, especially in an argument, of keeping his eyes closed until he finished speaking; Madalyn was intimidated by that, as if lightning bolts were being sharpened behind his lids. Moritz had not intimidated her. He will be saying to himself, I wish I hadn't talked so much! "You don't have to think that," she said to herself. "You don't have to think that," she said once more. "You don't have to think that, Moritz. Moritz, Moritz." Maybe she would give him a nickname. Moe or More or Morris or Less. He had a scar under his ear, a thin inch-long line along his jaw. Had she been that close to his face? His eyes had flitted across her face, but when she spoke, his eyes had been trained on her mouth.

She had never been at this place on the Danube Canal before. She could just as well have been standing beside a river in some other big city. She hadn't known that there were poplars growing down here. Once she had been to Milan with her parents. She couldn't remember what the occasion was. It wasn't a vacation; on vacation they went to Croatia or Sardinia. She had never been to another big city except Milan. It was before she started school. She only knew Vienna, and in Vienna she knew almost nothing. It smelled like the sea here. Probably all large bodies of water smelled like this. Near the Prater it smelled like burnt almonds and beer. Moritz slept with his cousin in the same room. He had told her so on the telephone. He lived at Number 4, Stuwerstrasse, only three minutes from the entrance to the Wurstelprater, the amusement park in the Prater. And in the basement of the house across the street there was some kind of church where every Sunday a black American preacher shouted about God and all kinds of other stuff, so loud you could hear it the whole length of the street even when your windows were closed. He had told her all that. How long had they talked on the telephone? Her phone card would be used up soon. What would she do then?

She strolled as far as the steps leading up to the Schwedenbrücke, which crossed the Danube Canal. She was being inundated by so many things and that's exactly what she had expected. That's why she wanted to be alone. But now she was sorry that he wasn't walking with her. If I met him again in an hour or two, that would be good, she thought. They hadn't arranged another meeting. But that didn't bother her. She felt free and relaxed and ready for anything. She felt like she did after a test when she knew she'd gotten a good grade.

It was cooler up on the street. A light wind was blowing. She was much too lightly dressed but she wasn't cold. Her hands were cold but she wasn't. They were cold like his hands. We have cold hands, she thought, both of us have cold hands. He hadn't said anything about her sweater, but she hadn't said anything about his jacket either. She knew she looked good in red and thought the yellow stripes were pretty. Maybe she would let her hair grow long again after all. On her cell phone display she saw it was already after four o'clock. The sun shone white behind white clouds. She could look directly at it without hurting her eyes. She was glad she didn't have girlfriends anymore. She didn't want to tell anyone about it. She resolved to walk through the city alone more often in the future, through neighborhoods she didn't know, Ottakring for example, through the run-down streets of the Turkish and Serbian neighborhoods and over to Mexikoplatz, if he would go with her. From the bridge she could see the place where they had stood.

First she thought she would take the U4 from Schwedenplatz to the Kettenbrückengasse, but then she decided to walk through town. By the subway station it smelled like pizza. There was a pizza stand there with big cola bottles and other trash strewn around. She was hungry. The smell of spicy melted cheese made her so ravenous she was dizzy, but pleasantly so. And as she passed a young man wearing black pants hanging halfway down his butt and eating pizza slices out of a cardboard box, she asked if he'd give her a piece. Without looking at her he said to go ahead and take one. He was chewing and holding a cigarette clamped between his ring finger and his little finger. She devoured the slice in three bites.

She could have another if she wanted, he said, again without looking at her. She said next time she saw him it would be her treat.

She remembered that she still had €3.30 in her pocket. She didn't think that at home they would notice the €2.30 missing from the cup in the kitchen cupboard or the fifty cents from her father's winter coat. How did Moritz pay for his cigarettes? He had tried to break into a cigarette machine.

"Moritz," she said. And then immediately "Moritz" again. For a half second she thought she had forgotten his name and was very shocked. Her stomach contracted. But soon it was okay again. She resolved to call him up as soon as she got home. She looked at his number but didn't push the green button. She just wanted to see the number. She saved it to her address book under Kaltenegger, Moritz; put a 0043 in front of the number, for Austria, so she could call him even from another country. I'm allowed to call him, she thought, because he's seven calls ahead of me. I wouldn't be compromising myself with him. He called me seven times, and all just because I talked to him at recess. Would he tell her some day how he had broken open a cigarette machine with his friends and what it had been like at the police station? Had he just gone to join those same friends? Would he tell them about her, that her name was Madalyn, a name no one else in Vienna had? She didn't care that he had done that thing with the cigarette machine. And she didn't care that he hadn't written the poem.

She walked along Franz Josef's Kai past the street sellers who spread their newspapers on the asphalt. It would be hip to buy a newspaper just to carry it under her arm, a newspaper in Arabic for example or French or best of all, in English. She could speak some English in case anyone addressed her. At the Aida pastry shop on the lower Rotenturmstrasse she bought a piece of cream cake and knew it wouldn't be enough. She gave herself time. She had time. Her mother wouldn't be home until six. She had never entered the inner city before from this direction. The first neon signs were blaring their messages against the sky.

It was as if Vienna was a different city.

Chapter Twelve

Her father was already home. That was unusual at five. He was in the kitchen putting ham and a piece of Emmental cheese onto a slice of black bread. He was wearing a suit and tie. That was also unusual. Normally, he changed as soon as he got home, slipping into jeans and a T-shirt and turning up the heat if the temperature was less than summery. And he wasn't wearing one of his usual gray suits but the black one that Madalyn had seen him wear only once or twice, a three-piece suit with patent leather shoes to match. He hugged his daughter, pressing her head against his chest. That was not unusual. He asked her to sit with him. He remained standing, however, holding the open face sandwich with his fingertips and leaning over the sink to bite into it. He had a big glass of milk to go with it. He asked where she had been. He'd been home more than an hour already and Mama would come home soon. His voice was not reproachful and he didn't seem particularly interested in the answer. He had a lot of gel in his hair and smelled strongly of aftershave, too strongly in Madalyn's opinion. Her father had two kinds of aftershave, one for everyday and one for special occasions. She didn't know when special occasions happened, but she had gotten him the good one for his birthday, in a perfume shop on the Graben at her mother's suggestion. Madalyn had contributed a bit to the purchase price from her allowance money.

"We've been invited out tonight," he said. He smiled. He'd been smiling the whole time.

"Me too?" asked Madalyn.

"No, no. You'd be bored to tears. Just Mama and me. We're going out to eat with some people. Mama saw a dress she liked downtown and has already tried it on a couple times. She's out buying it now."

The thought of being alone that evening was a big relief to Madalyn. *Who Wants to Be a Millionaire?* with Armin Assinger was on TV. They frequently watched it together. That was usually nice. She sat between Mama and Papa and because she often made funny comments about the contestants, she got a lot of appreciation. Today she wouldn't have wanted to do that. The very thought of sitting in front of the television with her parents – between them – gave her a panic attack.

"So why did you make yourself a sandwich ahead of time?"
"So I'm not so hungry in the restaurant."
"Why don't you want to be hungry if you're going out to eat?"
"I prefer to watch the others eat and just eat a little myself."

Her mother came home with two shopping bags and disappeared into the bathroom without talking to Madalyn. When she came out again it was dark outside. Her father was impatient and Madalyn was too. She could have screamed she was so impatient.

When the two of them were gone, Madalyn got her bike out of the bicycle room in the cellar and rode through town to the Danube Canal. She rode onto the Schwedenbrücke, locked her bike to the bridge railing with the chain, ran down the steps and walked some way along the river until she got to LESS. The giant painting was illuminated by a streetlight and its white shimmered majestically. He chose a good place, she thought. And she thought, why LESS? What does he mean when he calls himself LESS? Even from up close she couldn't decide whether the letters under the big white ones said *is novb*, *is movd*, or *is morb*. In the right lower corner of the picture, at eye level, there was something else, something too small to be seen from the other side of the Danube Canal, but now she could read it clearly: FOR CLAUDIA.

Chapter Thirteen

She felt like she was going to throw up. She had forgotten something, and now it stood clear in her memory. A hiccup, and it was there. That day and the preceding days rearranged themselves into a new image, as if photographed from another balcony: she had forgotten that she'd already known for a long time who Moritz was, that she had probably seen him often in the schoolyard and on the street too. Long before she had spoken to him at the Rahlstiege, she had known his face, his posture, and his clothes that were always the same. She had just forgotten. She thought she had even spoken to him once. He's the one that had asked her, outside the chemistry lab a month or so ago, where he could find the principal. She had forgotten him. Seen him, forgotten him, seen, forgotten. And why was she suddenly not going to forget him again? She had pushed one Moritz aside when the other one arrived – the one she was in love with before she had even met him. What if the two were not the same? He was the one caught breaking into a cigarette machine, the one her whole class – with one exception– was interested in, as if he had committed a crime in a movie, side-by-side with Denzel Washington and Johnny Depp and not, in reality, at the Südbahnhof. *She* had been the exception. *She* had not been interested in him. His hair had been longer. She saw him in her mind's eye standing before her, slouching, his pants pulled way down, not really handsome, crooked somehow, with one hand flat on his head and the skin on his neck reddened: "Got any idea where the principal's office is?" How would she not have an idea where the principal's office was after having been in this school for four years! But he couldn't know that. Had he thought she might be somebody like him? And that's why he asked her and nobody else? And didn't his face have a hardness to it that had now disappeared? The rumor was – she now recalled – that he was provisionally accepted at the school for a trial month, but under observation, and he had to report to the principal every day and to the police once a week. It had been a subject of debate. She had spoken out against admitting someone like him to the Rahlgasse school. He'd been expelled from another Gymnasium and what was any different here than in that school? It was against the "principle of equal treatment" (that was her father's opinion and she had reproduced it, precisely imitating him in gesture and tone of voice). And now she recalled, as clearly as if watching herself on a screen, the way she had stood with Bea Haintz and the others outside the classroom and someone had said, "That's him." He had come up the stairs behind everyone else, his hands buried in the pockets of his jacket with the Red Bull colors. His head was down and the smell of cigarette smoke trailed behind him. He had glanced over at them, coolly pulled one hand out of his pocket, and waved at them with his thumb and forefinger—aimed at them, actually—and grinned. And she had thought there was nothing, absolutely nothing, interesting about him except that his neck wasn't so red anymore and his hair had been trimmed. She also knew who Claudia was – had seen her, forgotten her, seen, forgotten – and of course also knew that she was in Moritz's class. She was a gymnast, a pretty good one. She'd competed for the school in gymnastics meets and represented Vienna in a meet in the Czech Republic, if Madalyn remembered right. But that was all she knew about her.

    She couldn't stand looking at the gigantic picture shimmering in the light of the street lamp anymore. She emitted a little squeak with each hiccup. She couldn't prevent it and it sounded bitterly funny. The dedication looked like it had been written in blood. On purpose? And if so, what purpose? Was blood supposed to mean forever? And then why would he call up another girl eight times in half an hour? She turned her back to the picture, sat down on the path right next to the canal, folded her arms on her knees, and sobbed. How could she have forgotten all that? Now the specialness had been drained from everything. When she spoke to him at recess – she looked at her watch in the light of the streetlamp and saw that it had been ten hours and forty-five minutes ago – he was the first and only Moritz and she was meeting him for the first time. As if at that moment he had extinguished all the others who were also him. And had been put there just for her. How else could she have known that that guy there was the one who had written the poem, a poem that he had not written at all? She had known: he's the one. It was written on his forehead and only she had the eyes to read it. But just a few days earlier, she had seen him in Gumpendorferstrasse with his arm around some girl's waist, a girl with very long, smooth blond hair, almost yellow. Now she knew that girl's name – it was written on the wall behind her, but she didn't know what to do.

She looked over at the Urania. In the darkness, she could no longer distinguish the wall from the path where they had ridden together. For a minute, half a minute, he had gotten on her nerves when he bent over her. If only she hadn't gotten annoyed! If only she had allowed him to put his head against hers! Now it was too late. It was her fault. The lights of the city shown up into the sky, the March air was hazy, and a group of young people were walking across the bridge, laughing shrilly. One of them was imitating another one; she wouldn't have wanted to be with them. The same thoughts kept returning, and each time, each thought hurt her as if for the first time, and each time each thought touched a place where she had not been hit or stabbed before. Why hadn't she brought her cell phone along! She would have called him from here. Standing in front of his picture. In front of "For Claudia." And then? What would she have said? The cold penetrated her jacket. Shivers ran up her hands and arms and across her shoulders and into her ribs and down her throat into her lungs. She coughed and her chest hurt. Her mouth twisted up in a way she never wanted it to because it made her look ugly. Other girls didn't have to work at being pretty. They were pretty and they could cry and were still pretty, could let themselves be seen by anyone at any moment and always stayed pretty. It hurt so much, so much, she didn't know what to do and didn't know where it hurt, where to press her fists against the hurt. She bent over and covered her face with her hands.

A man and woman stopped beside her and asked if there was anything wrong; could they help her?

"Why?" asked Madalyn.

"Did you take something?" asked the woman.

"No, nothing," said Madalyn. "I was just looking at the water." Her voice was calm and deep, as if someone else was speaking for her. She had thought she couldn't control her voice and that the only thing left was to choose between screaming and silence. She immediately gave it another try: "I'm waiting for my sister," a voice that came out of her mouth said, a voice like the voiceover in a nature film. "She'll be right back. She's walking the dog. I wanted to stay here. It's so beautiful when spring comes."

"It's a little cold," said the woman. She was obviously suspicious about the situation. "You might get a chill in your bladder sitting there."

Madalyn stood up. "It's okay. She'll be back soon anyway." She had the urge to keep talking, to tell about her non-existent dog, about her non-existent sister, that there were four of them at home, including two brothers, and that their parents had died in a car crash just a week ago.

The woman turned around once more to look at her. Madalyn didn't stick out her tongue at her. She said some nonsense out loud to herself and listened to her voice. It sounded like it didn't belong to her. The hiccups were gone but occasional tears still fell from her eyes. The wishes that had floated above her came clattering down one after the other, like blocks. The great block of longing – shattered; the little block of future – when we would have gone together to buy a jacket for me (she still had a birthday gift certificate from last year) – shattered; the never-bored-again-block (the first thing she thought when she saw Moritz standing by the steps was that she would never be bored again) – shattered; and what could have been love and simply had not yet emerged from its chrysalis – shattered. But after not so very many minutes, her imagination had become as calm as her voice and she almost felt like the person she had been twenty-four hours ago. That was the trick of talking out loud to herself. She could talk grammatically correct nonsense at lightning speed and she deployed that talent against fear, sadness, and unbearable joy.

She stood up and covered the evil name on the wall with her hands. Then she left, feeling heavy and very tired.

She unlocked the chain from her bike. Her fingers were clammy. The day had been warm. The sun had been warm. When she went to Frau Jeller's bookstore, the sun had shone on her left shoulder and her neck, and she had felt grown-up, like a woman with a goal and without any doubt that she would reach it. Now it was cold and a metallic smell rose from the canal. She walked her bike across the bridge, thinking, My bike doesn't know it yet, and at the same time thinking, That young woman with a goal and no doubts would never have such a stupid thought. Her own happiness disgusted her because it was over; it got smaller and smaller with every step. And that's why she started to walk somewhat slower. She wasn't the Madalyn of twenty-four hours ago, no. She didn't want to be her; but she didn't want to be who she was now either. She looked for a Madalyn in her memory, a good Madalyn she could and would transform herself into. "It's not that easy," she said out loud. "It's not that easy, unfortunately."

Her voice was completely under control again. It wasn't as interesting as it had been a little while ago. It was hers. Why shouldn't he be allowed to dedicate his picture to a girl he knew before he knew me! But tomorrow he's going to be sitting with her in the same class again.

When she got to the other side of the river (to the place where in a happier time someone had given her two slices of pizza), she didn't get on her bike as she had planned. It was so boring to ride a bike. But even if I walk all the way across town, she thought, I'll still get home much too early – before she was dead tired, before her parents got home. Should I walk the bike across the Ring and through the Stadtpark? Her mother had forbidden her to go into the park after dark. Or should I walk around town a little and look at the shop windows? She didn't want to talk to her parents. There was no thought she could look forward to, no topic she would have wanted to concentrate on even for a moment, no shop window that interested her. But she didn't want to be alone either. Alone in the apartment – the very thought shook her. Why did he show me a picture he'd made for someone else?

She turned around and rode back across the bridge and on into the second district. She pulled the sleeves of her jacket over her hands.

Chapter Fourteen

She rode toward the Prater. Two men were smoking under a red neon sign in front of a bar. She asked them where Stuwerstrasse was; did they know? The men didn't understand her. They looked at her with what seemed like indignant expressions. They were much older than they'd looked from far away. She pulled in her head and continued on, walking her bike. It had no headlight. She had forgotten to take along the battery-powered lamp that clipped to either your handlebars or your bike helmet. She more or less knew how to get to the Prater. She had often gone there from the center of town, but always with her parents and always in daylight. She had also heard that there was a neighborhood called the Stuwerviertel but didn't know if that had anything to do with the street of the same name. But she did know that it was a red-light district. She forced herself not to talk to her bicycle, though she would have liked to. The thoughts were no longer dancing around wildly in her head. All that was left was a burning pressure in her chest and she wouldn't have been able to say whether it was an illness or just her imagination.

She turned into a side street. It was quiet here; no one was out on the street. And it was dark. Most of the streetlights weren't working. Very little light came from the windows. She had on some crêpe-soled shoes that she hadn't liked at all at first, but now she did. If she had liked them right away she could have been the first girl to wear ankle-high, blood-red suede shoes with off-white soles. She couldn't hear her own steps. That was eerie, so she handled her bike roughly in order to make some sound. The street curved away into the distance and that confused her. I've got to remember this curve, she thought. On the telephone, Moritz had said that Stuwerstrasse was a side street off of Venediger Au. She couldn't remember having asked him. Assuming she had *not* asked, which was very probable, why had he told her about where he lived? Did he want her to come over? And what about her? Had she told him where she lived? She couldn't remember. Possibly yes. What if he was on his way to her house at that moment, just as she was on her way to his? She didn't believe he was. It was not a matter of indifference to her that she couldn't believe it. What she gave was always more than what she got. Why? Why should that be? In the fifth grade she had a crush on a girl named Laura Fuhrmann. She had black hair like an animal's pelt and eyes black as a dream and Madalyn wanted to be with her every day. She even wanted to sleep at her house but she wasn't allowed to. She was never bored when they were together, but at some point Laura said that she didn't want to be with her anymore for a while, but with another girl. Whereupon Madalyn wrote her a letter which she saw fall out of Laura's English book a few days later and she could see that it hadn't even been opened yet.

What was the Venediger Au? A part of the Prater? A park? A public housing project? An avenue? Now she was no longer able to get her bearings. She couldn't see the outline of the giant Ferris wheel between the houses anymore. She didn't know where she was. Had no idea which direction she was going. Or where St. Stephen's Cathedral was. Not even where the Danube Canal was. It was as if she was really in a different city – like the one she had conjured up in her imagination that afternoon, that happy afternoon. It would have been so beautiful to get to know this Vienna with him. Who had called it "this Vienna"? Did the boys he hung out with say "this Vienna"? It sounded like a device you could use for something, a tool for doing bad things. She retraced her steps. Nothing here seemed familiar. But she had been walking on this sidewalk just a minute ago! The street was only dimly lit. Her father had said that the new energy-saving streetlights would lead to more suicides because the light was so depressing. She got on her bike and started pedaling furiously down the street and across the next one, and it made her feel less lonely.

She reached a four-lane road with cars traveling at high speed. Now she could see the giant Ferris wheel again. At this time of year it wasn't illuminated and stood motionless, nothing but a thin circle with thick, dark chunks – the individual cabins – outlined against the sky. When the light turned green she rode across the intersection and straight toward Venediger Au. So Venediger Au was a street whose right side ran along the Prater park with its tall trees just beginning to leaf out. The second cross street was Stuwerstrasse. She stopped and walked her bike slowly onto that street, ready at any moment to turn around and ride away if anything happened. On the left side, she saw the sign that said in English that this was a church; in the windows hung colorful pictures of Jesus with a halo, all the same, differing only a little in their colors. Jesus stood between the window frames in a long robe with many folds, his arms spread wide and rays of light shining from his hands. In the gloom they looked like monstrous fingernails. Diagonally across the street was Number 4 and on the ground floor, just as Moritz had said, there was a Thai massage parlor, actually called the Institute for Energetics as she could read above the greasy yellow windows.

The doorbells at the entrance were illuminated. There was no one named Kaltenegger. His aunt's name probably wasn't Kaltenegger anymore. After all, she was married, had been married, or was divorced from her husband. Did he tell me that on the telephone too? Was her name Konzett or Ümit or Tömördi? She couldn't make out some of the names because they were written in ink that had run or in pencil that had faded.

She parked her bike and went to the other side of the street and folded her arms and rubbed her hands up and down because in the meantime, she had become quite chilly. The lights were on in all the windows of the building. What else had he told her? That he slept in the same room as his cousin. It could be any of these windows. Was his cousin younger or the same age or older? Did they get along? She thought hard to see if anything else occurred to her. Had he said at some point what he saw when he looked out of the window? Maybe his window looked onto the rear courtyard. She crossed the street again and tried the front door. It had a knob that didn't turn. What had he said about his aunt? Nothing. Except that she had a boyfriend. If she lived here with her boyfriend, both their names were probably next to the doorbell. One of the little signs written with ink looked like there were two names on it. Of course, it could also be a first and last name. She rested her finger on that button. And what if it was the right one? What if Moritz's voice came through the intercom? In that case, it would be easy; she would say, This is Madalyn. If she dared. But she was pretty sure she wouldn't. But would she even recognize his voice? He would probably not say more than Yes? If it was his aunt's boyfriend or she wasn't sure if it was the boyfriend or Moritz, would she say, Is Moritz there? And what if he wasn't? She would think, He's at Claudia's. She would think that in any case. She knew herself. She couldn't get it out of her head and she would imagine all sorts of things; she knew herself. She didn't think she could stand it. She closed her eyes tight. But it was already in her head. She might as well push the button. Once more, she went to the other side of the street. The windows were lit, all of them, but nothing moved behind any of them. At least, nothing she could see. Which windows went best with his aunt? How should she know? He hadn't said anything about her. Except that she had two children and a boyfriend and had taken in her nephew when he didn't want to live with his father anymore. She must be a nice woman, she thought, otherwise she would never have done that. And her boyfriend was nice too. Moritz had said so explicitly. The probability that a nice man had a nice girlfriend was greater than the probability that he had one who wasn't nice. So the aunt was probably a nice woman. But how could she tell from the curtains if a person was nice or not? The windows on the top floor were blank, without curtains. They don't live there, she thought. The way she imagined Moritz's aunt, she was also a warm person. Only a warm person, she thought, has two children of her own and then takes in her nephew too. Because it's stressful, after all, and only a warm person would have the nerve to do it. And a warm person is likely to have curtains in her windows. On the next floor down, each window was different: red curtains, sheer white curtains. Behind the one farthest to the left, Venetian blinds with narrow red vanes had been lowered unevenly, halfway down. She thought she could see the corner of a picture frame and, if she wasn't mistaken, a potted plant, but it could also have been a piece of clothing hanging from the window frame. That was his room, she decided. The windows on the second story all looked the same: light curtains, all closed. No, no, he lives on the third floor and the left-hand window is his room.

Maybe it was possible to approach the house from behind. She rode to the Venediger Au and then past some buildings and into the next cross street. But here too, there was an unbroken row of attached houses. She pushed tentatively on an entrance gate. There was no chance of getting into the inner courtyard. She picked up a stone, put it in her pocket, and rode back to Stuwerstrasse. In the stucco next to the entrance of Number 4 she scratched two letters no taller than half her little finger: M M.

Chapter Fifteen

Her parents were already back home. They were beside themselves. Her father was a little drunk. Madalyn noticed it because he was speaking slower and quieter than usual, but also more than usual, and he was getting muddled, and mostly repeating what her mother said, at least at first. Her mother had already taken off her new dress. She was barefoot and had on a slip with thin straps. Which meant that what she said couldn't be true, namely, that she had been about to go out into the night to look for Madalyn. She pressed her fists together against her chest, thrust her elbows forward so that her upper body looked hollow and distorted, like a compressed spring about to be released. The muscles on her upper arms stood out and on the skin of her cheeks appeared the little wrinkles that were a sure sign she was furious. Madalyn knew what she was in for. She undid her shoes, taking her time, gazing at the shoes she had bought with her mother in a shoe store next to St. Stephen's Cathedral. Her mother stood over her, scolding away. This would be just the beginning. Soon she would instinctively find the place that hurt the most. But Madalyn wasn't afraid. Her mother could be really mean. Her father didn't repeat the mean things. He was scolding her too, but in his own words, and they were no longer directed at Madalyn, but at his wife, as if he was trying to say, It works this way too, why don't you do it like I do, then you can back out of it more easily later on. Her mother said things that were difficult to forgive, in fact, could only be forgiven if Madalyn didn't listen. That was something she had learned. And she succeeded this time too, by using her nonsense method. She talked nonsense in her head, but her lips moved. It didn't work otherwise. Her mother thought she was imitating her because Madalyn imitated everything. And so her mother started screaming. It was a quiet screaming. Madalyn had often tried to imitate this quiet screaming. But that was the one thing she had never succeeded at. It was easy to imitate her father, but not her mother. Her father clapped his hands twice and said they might as well, all of them, stop this now. It was an excellent idea, wasn't it, to stop right now? Didn't they think so? Nothing had happened so far, why get excited when nothing had happened? Madalyn was still fingering her shoes and moving her lips. Her mother screamed for her to stand up. Her father said that as far as he was concerned it was all over. He had been worried about her, and he had a right to be. He did blame her, however, for ruining the end of their evening like this. Because they had had a really nice time. His voice couldn't compete with his wife's and didn't even try to. He was starting to get on Madalyn's nerves and on her mother's too. If I stand up, thought Madalyn, she'll shake me by the shoulders. But I'm not going to cry. Not that she suddenly had the strength to suppress her crying, because she didn't. It just didn't hurt her the way her mother was talking, not this time, and not what she was saying, not this time. The angry words and the angry tone flew past her like poorly aimed arrows. She felt a little sick to her stomach. They were still in the entrance hall of the apartment. Madalyn, squatting, saw her parents' legs in front of her, her mother's athletic calves and her father's elegant pants and shoes, and she felt a little ill. It had to do with her mother's voice, that was all. Sometimes she felt a little ill when listening to music. How am I going to put up with this until I'm sixteen? If she was afraid of anyone, it was of herself. And her throat was hurting a little too. And her head. Now her father took her mother by the upper arms and shook her. She was going too far, he said. He didn't want one member of the family saying things like that to another member, no matter who and no matter to whom. Madalyn hadn't been listening. She took the opportunity to stand up. What had her mother said?

"Where were you?" asked her father, looking into her face for the first time; for the first time in a long time, to tell the truth.

"I went for a walk," she said.

Her mother tore herself free from her father, ran into the kitchen, and came back with a plastic bag. She held it in front of her mouth. She did that when she was so furious that she was afraid of hyperventilating. In a peaceful hour Madalyn had asked her mother how that worked. How can it be good to breathe into a bag when you were afraid of suffocating? Her mother was hoarse already. Madalyn was familiar with that to.

"I just went for a walk," she said again. "That's all. It was just a walk." On purpose she spoke quite softly. She knew that her mother definitely wanted her to say something so she'd have something to flail away at and get even more hoarse. To have another thing to hold against her. For a moment they were all silent. With a rasping sound, her mother inhaled her own breath from the plastic bag from the Hofer supermarket. "I couldn't stand being alone," Madalyn whispered, and before her mother could start in again, she added quickly, "Nobody else in my class is alone as much as me." And she lied, "That's exactly what we're supposed to write an essay on next week." She didn't expect it to make an impression on her mother.

It didn't make an impression on her mother.

Her mother breathed quickly in and out into the plastic bag, turned to the side and said, "I never wanted to have a child." And she said to her husband, "Tell her, it's true!"

"Then return me," said Madalyn.

It just came to her to say that. She thought it was good. She didn't make the mistake of repeating it. It would have been just half as hurtful. She wished she could repeat it so that it would only be half as hurtful. And repeat it again: a fourth. And again: an eighth. It pained her to have said such a thing. But she did think it was good, too. She could no more take it back than her mother could take back what she had said, and not just today, but repeatedly. Now Madalyn had said something similar. It may have been the first time she said something she couldn't take back. It was like being in New York for the first time. Or smoking your first cigarette. The only possible way to calm her mother down would be to cry. But she couldn't. Although it was one of her specialties to pretend to be crying. When she really cried she produced fewer tears then when she fake cried. She could imitate the way people cried whom she had never seen cry. She knew how her father cried although he had never cried in front of her. She was one hundred percent sure she knew how Moritz cried. She wished he would cry once in front of her. He will some day, he will, and he'll be happy to have done it in front of me. Moritz had argued with his father. We'll talk about that, him and me. He wants to talk to me. I know he wants to. He called up eight times in a half hour. He painted that picture days ago. It doesn't count anymore. She had no aunt she could move in with. Maybe she could move in with his aunt, with the nice, warm woman on Stuwerstrasse, Stuwerstrasse, Stuwerstrasse. All I know is, green grass on fire escapes that grow from the carpet like the titmice in Kenya with the Turkish roses from the clouds by night. She moved her lips and looked her mother in the eye.

"What did you say?" Her mother didn't remove the plastic bag from her mouth.

"Nobody here means what they say right now," her father asserted as if it were a fact.

"May I go to bed?" Madalyn asked.

"What do you mean, I should take you back?" her mother persisted.

"I didn't mean it."

"Madalyn," said her father. "Madalyn!" He could say her name so it sounded as if it contained the whole world and all his love. But she didn't believe him. Any second her mother was going to say "Madi."

She said it.

Madalyn closed her eyes and there was a darkness before her that she hadn't expected. Down by the Danube Canal they had talked about smoking cigarettes. That occurred to her. He had said that when he closed his eyes after his first cigarette in the morning, it was darker than on the darkest night. He liked that. When tomorrow comes, I'm going to smoke a cigarette. I'm going to smoke a cigarette with him. She closed her eyes again. This time it wasn't so dark.

"May I please go to bed?"

"Who were you with?" asked her mother. Her voice was only a hiss, but it wasn't a mean hiss.

"Nobody."

"Something's going on, I can tell. Something's different, I can feel it!"

"I just went for a walk, really."

Madalyn knew what her mother meant. There were no tears. She herself found it unsettling that there were no tears. Without her daughter's tears, her mother would not be able to find her way out of her anger. She wouldn't let her go to her room. Madalyn tried. It wasn't necessary to think of something sad. One time one of her classmates wanted Madalyn to teach her how to cry. To cry at the drop of a hat. Here's how Madalyn did it: she thought about a movie in which somebody is crying. People cried in a lot of movies. Almost every movie had somebody who was crying. She memorized the crying face and then imitated it. That was all. And it worked this time, too.

"Don't cry," said her father.

"I'm sorry, Madi," said her mother. "I was crazy with worry. Do you understand?"

"I'm sorry too, Mama."

"So you understand?"

"Yes, I understand."

Madalyn went to her room. And locked the door behind her. Nobody pounded on the door.

Chapter Sixteen

"Where are you, Moritz?"

"At home. In the stairwell."

"What're you doing in the stairwell?"

"I tried calling you a hundred times."

"Ten times, only ten. I can see it on my screen."

"Where were you, Madalyn?"

"You wouldn't believe me anyway."

"Come on, tell me."

"At your house."

"What do you mean, at my house?"

"I was in front of your house."

"On Stuwerstrasse?"

"Yeah, Moritz."

"Why didn't you call me?"

"I was looking at your picture by the Danube Canal. From up close. You painted it for Claudia."

"I added *For Claudia* later. The picture is much older."

"I don't believe you."

"It's not important, Madalyn."

"I bet it's important for her."

"You always write something. Every sprayer writes who the picture is for. Everybody does it."

"Don't say that. There's nothing on the other pictures."

"I can paint over it. By tomorrow somebody else may have sprayed over the picture anyway, more likely than not."

"Which window is yours?"

"What do you mean, on Stuwerstrasse?"

"Let me guess. You live on the third floor and your window is the one with the red blinds, right?"

"How did you know that?"

"What's going on with Claudia, Moritz? I mean now. What's going on between you and her?"

"That ended a while ago."

"I don't believe you."

"But now there's nothing going on. I swear it. I've fallen in love with you, Madalyn. What else can I say. I wasn't really in love with Claudia, I was just with her. I love you. I was never really in love before. I fell in love with you on the spot. That's why I keep coming out to the stairwell, because I can't really telephone in the apartment. Cause they always want to know who I'm talking to. I'm in love with you, Madalyn. If you don't believe anything else I say, you have to believe that, please."

"Do I have to? If I have to, I will."

"You have to believe that I love you."

"Okay, I believe you."

"What about you?"

"I rode my bike to Stuwerstrasse."

"If you'd had your cell phone along, I wouldl have come outside and we could have walked around and talked. Tell me: do you love me too? Do you, Madalyn? Tell me, Madalyn!"

She didn't say it. Not because she didn't want to. She would have liked to tell him. But she wasn't a machine.

"I'm not a machine," she said.

After she hung up she was sorry she hadn't said it. She really would like have liked to say it to him, but not as an answer to his question. It would have been too little, it would have been only a half. The question one half, the answer the other half. When I see him in school tomorrow I'll and go right up and whisper it in his ear. Before he says it to me, I'll say it to him.

But then she wrote a text message and told him after all. And she got a text message back in which he told her.

She put on her pajamas, unlocked her door, and went into the hall. It was quiet in the apartment. The lights had been turned off. She went to the kitchen, took a yogurt out of the refrigerator, dribbled some syrup on it, and spooned it into her mouth. She sat there for a while, her feet pulled up and her arms hugging her legs. Secretly she hoped that at that very moment, LESS was being painted over. LESS scurried through her thoughts as a restless spirit, breeding lies. Did he have a photo of Claudia? She could try spraying a picture herself some time. She stood up, pulled the curtains aside, and looked at the roof across the street, a large, gray surface that lost itself in shadows and fog to the right and left. Her father was a man with ingratiating eyes and a soft mouth. A man who was always well dressed. And for her, always a little spooky. And he smelled good. Always. She felt as she did sometimes when she lay in the tub and no one was at home and she had finished her homework and emptied the dishwasher. Outside it would still be light for a long time and she was looking forward to something, nothing specific, just to a dream that caused her no hesitation, because everything in it was her own invention.

She sat there for a while. Finally she slipped into her parents' bedroom and crawled into bed between her mother and her father. Her mother woke up and pulled the blanket over Madalyn's shoulders.

"I'm so sorry, Madi," she whispered. "So, so sorry! Forgive me, forgive me, forgive me, forgive me one last time, forgive me, Madi, just one more time!"

"Can I sleep in your bed tonight?" Madalyn asked.

"Cuddle up to my back," her mother said and turned over. She reached back and took Madalyn's hand and drew it to her mouth and kissed it.

What does *I was just with her* mean, thought Madalyn. I should have asked him. She wanted to get out of bed and go to her room and try calling Moritz. But then she fell asleep.

Chapter Seventeen

And yet the days before Frau Petri's class went to Weimar were beautiful days for Madalyn. I say *and yet*, because in those almost two weeks her heart – and this is my interpretation, a conclusion I drew from what she told me – found no peace and her thoughts no refuge. She had not been a single minute without turmoil and anxiety, had woken up several times every night with clenched fists and furrowed brow and felt no interest whatever in the world. And besides, in those two brief weeks she had done many things she had never done before, things she would never have imagined doing.

"And yet it was a happy time?" I asked.

"The happiest time of my life," she answered and repeated it and said it a third time while giving me a challenging look, as if I had a desire or the power to destroy the magic of the sentence and convert her memories into something dark – which in my opinion some of them were. But I'm not a spoilsport, not even if I have some reservations about the sport. I don't have to play if I don't want to. – That's what I thought as we sat in Neni's restaurant.

"The next day, after the long recess," she continued her story, "Moritz and I agreed we would sign ourselves out of school. We both gave the same excuse. We had also agreed on that. We said we had a stomach ache and felt nauseated." – That had been his idea, not hers. Madalyn had never played hooky. It had been her idea for them to both plead the same excuse.

They left school separately so they wouldn't be seen together. At the Secession building she got on his bicycle. He had brought along a cushion in his backpack so she could ride more comfortably. He had made a detailed plan for the morning. They rode through the center of town straight to the Danube Canal and with her as witness, he sprayed yellow paint over the words *For Claudia*. She tried to push his hand aside. She didn't want him to do that. He said it was a pledge of his love. Those were his actual words. It occurred to her during recess that she had forgotten to say the words into his ear that he would have liked so much to hear but had only read as a text message. They had been too busy organizing their escape. And besides, she imagined that she had seen the girl with the smooth yellow hair looking over at them, and she imagined that Moritz had seen her too. Now, she didn't want to say it, not at this moment. He would think it was some kind of thanks or something. But she was not grateful to him for anything, especially not for spraying over a name on a wall. Even if he had extinguished that name from his head, please and thank-you would not have been called for.

When Madalyn woke up that morning, her first thought was: I can't be mad at that Claudia, and I can't be mad at Moritz either, and I hope Claudia isn't mad at me. She'd have more reason to be than me – maybe I can be her friend and she can be mine. That last thought emerged from her almost automatically, as a logical continuation; she didn't believe it for a second. But the thought had spread a kind of malice over her other thoughts and she felt uncomfortable, like a liar, spraying her false colors in all directions. She told herself that people very seldom remain with their first love their whole lives. Most people, when they finally find someone they're going to stay with for the rest of their lives, have already put several loves behind them. She even remembered having heard somewhere, probably on afternoon TV, that it was absolutely not a good idea to have had only one love in your life; such a person becomes diminished and loses their beauty more quickly and becomes bitter in old age. At the same time however, she felt –and felt it without the slightest doubt – that she would never want any other person in her life than Moritz Kaltenegger, felt it even though, strangely enough, she again had to work hard to remember what he looked like. She could describe his mouth, could have drawn a picture of it, his nose, his eyes, his hair that always looked wet somehow, his clothes too of course. She could have described exactly how he leaned forward when he had something important to say, how he leaned forward when he lit a cigarette. But she was not able to see his image in her mind's eye. It was like reading music. She had taken violin lessons for two years. She knew all the notes, all the time signatures and dynamic markings, but musical notation had never coalesced as melody in her head. That was the reason why her violin teacher had advised her parents to allow her to stop. At breakfast, there had been a buzzing lightness inside her like after an illness, and when she remembered how she had raced over into the second district last night on her bicycle and had hung around in front of Number 4 Stuwerstrasse, she felt as though she really was sick. He had *just been with her.* Nothing special. The special thing would be if they had slept with each other. After breakfast, she again felt like she was going to throw up. Her parents were being so nice to her that that had finally calmed her down. There should have been two Madalyns: one her parents scolded and another who cashed in on their bad conscience the next day; everyone in the world would rather be the second.

Moritz had brought some spray cans along, one with yellow paint, one with red, and one with green. With the yellow one he painted over *For Claudia*. With the green one he wanted to spray *For Madalyn* and with the red one add a few rays around it so everyone would notice it right away. But Madalyn didn't want him to. She didn't want her name on the wall, not next to this picture, not under any circumstances. He could see that she was serious and he let it go. And didn't ask why.

"I'll spray a new one just for you," he said. "Bigger than this one here. Not LESS, but something new. This one won't be here long anyway. I know a guy who's hot to paint over it because it's a good location. He asked me. He's going to give me a couple of cans in exchange. I already made some drawings yesterday, filled up half the notebook. But I'm not going to show them to you. It's going to be the best thing I ever sprayed. By far."

Now would have been the time to whisper in his ear. Again, however, he might have thought it was a kind of thank-you.

Moritz said he wanted to show her something else, not graffiti but something different.

Chapter Eighteen

On Nestroyplatz he bought them muffins and Coke and they took the bike onto the U1 subway. When they reached the Old Danube, Madalyn got on the crossbar again and they rode along the path by the water, past the weekend houses whose shutters were closed because it was a Tuesday morning on the last day of March and there was no reason for anybody to drive out here from the city. This time she didn't draw back when he put his cheek next to hers. She pressed her head against it and they rubbed their cheeks against each other. He said that everything he had told her last night was true. As soon as we stop, she thought, I'll whisper in his ear.

There was an old house that looked like a villa. It was a wooden house, painted turquoise, with ornamental window frames. The paint was peeling off and the windows were boarded up. Behind the boards the panes were so dusty you couldn't see through them. On the sides of the house there were little towers, like watchtowers, that were topped by weathervanes. In the front was a wide porch of rotting planks that had been broken through in several places. Moritz chained the bike to a lamp post a little distance from the house and climbed over the fence.

"You could do it by yourself," he said, "but I'll help you."

"I don't think this is a good idea," she said.

"Nobody cares," he said. "It's been standing empty for a year."

"I don't think it's a good idea," she said again. "It's breaking and entering. Don't do it, Moritz!" But then she did it, and it went pretty easily.

He said he'd been here a lot. He didn't say if he'd come alone or with somebody else and she preferred not to ask. One of the windows at the shady backside of the house could be shoved open a little, wide enough to reach in and press down the latch of the back door.

The house smelled musty – of rot, mildew, and rat droppings. It was better upstairs Moritz said. And it was nicely furnished – a big room with little round tables like in a coffeehouse and with leather chairs and two sofas. There were shelves built into the walls but no books left. The windows, through which only a little light filtered, were hung with long velvet drapes that were gray with dust and ragged along the bottom edge. In the middle of the room a staircase led to the next floor. You could tell by the colors of the steps that there had been a runner. It too had been removed.

"Whose house is it?" Madalyn asked.

"No idea."

"What if they come back?"

"We'd be faster."

"You're joking, right?"

On the third floor there were three small rooms and a bathroom. They only peeked in at the doors. In the rooms were bare mattresses and nothing else. They sat down on the steps and had their muffins and Coke.

"I don't know anything about you, hardly," she said.

He asked if she would like a beer. He had made himself a cache, he said, grinning. There were a few bottles covered with newspaper in a niche next to a box.

"Do you come here often?" she asked.

"Sometimes."

He opened a bottle with his lighter, took a swallow, and handed it to her. She had never drunk beer. Sometimes her mother drank a glass with lunch, only a small glass; rarely did she drink a second one, but when she did, then also a third and a fourth and told funny stuff, like recently, when she said that as a child she had breathed against the window panes in the winter to see the delicate branchings that formed on the cold glass, and that she had been addicted to them. The smell of beer nauseated Madalyn. But she took swallow. They passed the bottle back and forth until it was empty. He lit a cigarette and asked if she wanted to have a drag too, and she put the cigarette briefly between her lips.

"I know what you're thinking," he said.

She would have liked to rinse out her mouth. She could feel the alcohol in the back of her neck. Her eyes were getting slow. "What am I thinking?"

"What they all think."

"What do they all think, Moritz?"

He held the empty bottle between his knees, played with it, stuck his finger in the opening and swung it back and forth. "That I *always* do bad things because I did something bad *once*."

"Breaking into a house is a bad thing," she said.

"It is if you steal something or break something. But I don't do that. Not at all. In fact, I even straighten things up. You should've seen what it used to look like in here. I know what you're thinking, Madalyn. You think I was here with Claudia. I wasn't. I was never here with anybody. When the police arrested me because of the cigarette machine, I didn't know what to do. I rode around on my bike all day. I thought, it's all over now, I'll never amount to anything. I thought that everybody would know everything about me. I felt like everybody was looking at me. And then I happened to ride by here and saw the house. I thought the house looked the way I felt. Nothing's going to become of this house anymore, I thought, just like me. I climbed the fence and went around to the back and saw the window and opened it, like today." – He lit another cigarette and blew the smoke far into the room. Scratching sounds could be heard. He said those were rats – rats or martens or mice. No, he'd never seen any. That's why he was smoking another one. They didn't like the smell. – "You've got stuff," he continued.

"You have a lot. I've got nothing. Just my school things and a few other clothes to wear. Do you have your own room?"

She nodded.

"If I want to be alone, I have to go into the stairwell. It's not so bad. I go up to the attic. Up there you can sit down and nobody sees you. I know what you're thinking, Madalyn."

"What am I thinking?"

"That it's all lies."

"That's not what I'm thinking, Moritz."

"I lie a lot. That's the truth. No one notices. Because I'm pretty good at it. For example, I lied to you yesterday, sorry. Really sorry."

He inclined his head toward her. She didn't want to know what the lie was. It wasn't one anymore. Her hand felt its own warmth in his.

He said, "This is really hard for me. I didn't really paint that picture." He squared his shoulders, rubbed his nose with the back of his hand, and took a deep breath.

She put her arms around his skinny body. "I don't care about that at all," she said quickly, not letting go of him.

"But I care!" He blurted out. "I care! With Claudia it didn't matter to me. But with you it does. Claudia was the only one in the class who was nice to me. I wanted to be a big shot in front of her and I just sprayed her name next to LESS. I don't know who painted LESS. Got no idea. She thinks I sprayed it for her. What do you say to that, Madalyn? I know what you're thinking. I can always tell what you're thinking."

That she was happy about it, that's what she was thinking. But she didn't want to tell him that. She took his face between her hands and kissed him on the mouth. She had never done that with anyone before. He had certainly done it with Claudia. But she was better at it than he was. And that made her happy.

Chapter Nineteen

That same day he also told her about his friends, and that they called him Rizzo. Madalyn said she thought it was a beautiful name, and asked if it was spelled with tz or with one z or with two. And they had agreed on two z's.

On that day, however, he didn't call her anymore. Her phone card was empty. Her mother had canceled their landline a year ago after getting a telephone bill for €532.40. She waited, standing at the window of her room and looking at the sky where there was nothing but a color that could go with any season. She drifted around the apartment, the moist, warm cell phone in her hand so she wouldn't miss the first ring, the first vibration, and she kept looking at the screen. She heard her parents' voices coming from all directions and would not have been able to say if they were speaking to her or to each other. When she saw the crows flying past her window, heading for their roosts on the Baumgartnerhöhe, she had a pain in her throat and her chest she thought she had never felt before. The piece of paper with the poem her mother had written out from memory was still there on the kitchen table. In the night she put the cell phone under her pillow. For when he wakes up and goes out to the stairwell, she thought. But he didn't call. He didn't call in the morning either. She took her cell phone to school, something she had not done for a long time. He's embarrassed to talk to me, she thought, embarrassed for all kinds of reasons. That seemed like a waste of time to her. Before class started she went up to his classroom. He wasn't there and Claudia wasn't there either, not in the classroom and not in the hall. That didn't necessarily mean anything. But maybe it did.

In the long recess she saw Claudia standing down in the schoolyard. And Madalyn could see that Claudia was just as worried as she was. At least she thought she could see that. And for a moment, it made her so happy that she would have liked to run up and give her a hug. The blond girl stood near the building wall that faced the school. She was alone, her back turned to the others and her head lowered, as if she was looking at something by her feet. Why hadn't he said anything more about her? All he said was that she was the only person in his class who was nice to him. All the others snubbed him. When he said it, he ducked his head as if he was getting noogies. But he was grinning like it had been an adventure. I'm one of the others, thought Madalyn, I snubbed him to. I hope no one remembers that. Hopefully no one will tell him. Maybe somebody already has.

On Friday they had a math test. Madalyn was getting a B in math, a pretty shaky B at that. She had put off studying, and now she really didn't feel like it. There was a long-standing plan to study with two of her classmates that afternoon. She had forgotten about it. They were going to meet at Madalyn's house and bring cake along. Madalyn said she still wasn't feeling well; she had thrown up twice that morning. Throwing up enjoyed a certain status in her class. It was clear to her that without studying she would flunk the test and then be getting a C-. Her mother would freak out even though she herself didn't know squat about math – even bragged about it at every opportunity. Madalyn canceled the date with her classmates.

She ran down to the schoolyard, gathered up her courage, touched the shoulder of the girl with long blond hair, and pulled back her hand at once.

"Can I ask you something?"

Claudia's eyelids fluttered briefly. She was holding the lapels of her coat together with one hand.

Did she know where Moritz Kaltenegger was?

Madalyn was unable to interpret her look. It could have been a look of triumph just as well as simple distraction. From close up, she looked different than Madalyn had expected; she couldn't decide whether she looked better or not so good, because at that moment her cell phone rang and she looked at the screen and saw it was Moritz but didn't dare to press the green connect button.

"Sorry – my mom," she said. The lie sounded lame.

Claudia didn't answer. She had remarkably hooded eyes, or she was making them look that way. Now she sucked one corner of her mouth into her cheek and looked like she was at least twenty and certainly not sad. Her lipstick was flaking in one place. Madalyn held the cell phone in her fist at arm's length to dampen its ring. A story started up in her head, the story of a deep, sympathetic relationship between Moritz and this girl who seemed to her a woman, an indestructible love from which he sometimes fled, but always returned and was always welcomed back. It was a plot in which she, Madalyn, was always the lover without a chance – a narrow universe of high school, cafeteria, and lowered blinds, a universe that vanished at once when she recognized it as an American movie she'd seen a few days ago on afternoon TV and thought was total crap.

Her cell phone stopped ringing.

"You were saying?" said Claudia.

Madalyn turned and ran back into the school and up the stairs; her only thought was to get away, far away, as far away as possible from the towering superiority of that face, which from close up was more beautiful than she had even imagined in her fear. That was now crystal clear. He called me up eight times, then ten times, and now once, and I've called him a total of twice. He won't call again. As if all was lost if she didn't reach him in the next few minutes. In that case she would run away and never come back to Vienna, she thought. She would do it this time. There was nothing exciting about this thought, only emptiness and a lack of color like last night in the sky. The door to the principal's office was open.

There was a coat lying on the desk. It lay there with its lining exposed. The corner of something in ribbed brown leather was sticking out of the breast pocket. Madalyn stepped in, pushed the door closed a little so she couldn't be seen from the hall, and took the wallet out of the pocket. There were several bills inside. She took a twenty, put the wallet back, and was out again. Nobody had seen her. She ran down the stairs and out of the building. There were five minutes of recess left. Up on Mariahilferstrasse was a tobacco store. She was lucky to be the only customer. She bought a telephone card for twenty euros. On the steps to the Rahlgasse she heard the school bell and took three steps at a time. When she entered the classroom, she was dizzy and gasping for breath. Frau Petri smiled at her and said she wanted to talk to her after class. Madalyn had forgotten that they had German fourth period. The teacher put her hands on Madalyn's shoulders as she often did. She only did it to Madalyn. She looked into her eyes and asked if anything was wrong. She hadn't been feeling well yesterday, said Madalyn. But she was better today.

As soon as she caught her breath, she said she had to go to the bathroom. Her stomach was hurting a little, she said softly.

In the bathroom, she entered the combination into her cell phone and pressed Moritz's number. He answered immediately. She wanted to speak first and talk in a strong deep voice from the beginning so she wouldn't sound so childish again, something she definitely didn't need at the moment. Why hadn't he called her yesterday, she asked. He hadn't called in the afternoon or in the evening or at night. And why wasn't he in school? She hadn't called him either, he countered, and his voice was harder than hers. He was expecting her to call, too. He had figured she thought he was a loser and didn't want anything to do with him anymore. He thought that was why she didn't call, because she thought he was a loser. Typical, he figured.

"Why typical?" she asked.

"Because you didn't believe anything I said. You didn't believe all the stuff I told you, right?"

"No, not right! That's totally wrong," she whispered into her cupped hand. She was afraid someone was going to burst through the door. "My telephone card was used up. I couldn't call. I forgot to tell you. It gets used up fast when I talk to you, and we talked for a long time. It's so stupid. It gets used up right away."

But now she was calling him, he said. Was she some kind of magician, or what? Telephone card magic, or what? And why didn't she pick up before? He especially called her during the long recess. He didn't feel like coming to school today. – His tone of voice was very rough. But that didn't bother her. He has to talk that way, she thought. He feels insulted. No way he can know what happened. And when you're insulted, that's how you talk. So now she told him. She even told him twice. Then there was a long silence between them.

"I thought you didn't like me," he said.

His voice was soft and higher. It was like a boy's voice, and for the second time within a few hours Madalyn thought about the delicate designs her mother, when she was little, had breathed onto the window panes in winter – his voice was like that. Now she had told him because of something other than pure feeling. She had said it so he wouldn't be insulted anymore and would talk to her in a different way, not so rough and cold. At the end of their conversation she would say it again, she told herself. I'll say ciao, he'll say ciao, and then I'll say it and hang up. It would be best to say it in the middle of a sentence when they were talking about something else some time – poems, or Africa, or beer and cigarettes. Then it would have been just right.

"I went to the Flex last night and got drunk," he said. – She didn't know what the Flex was. – "I thought I'd ruined everything.

Not by lying, but because I didn't lie. I thought it would have been better if I'd lied. I don't want to lie to you, Madalyn. I thought, now I've paid the price. Should've lied like always."

It was urgent that she get back to class. Frau Petri would come to see what was wrong if she stayed away so long. She liked Frau Petri a lot but she didn't like it that the teacher treated her so solicitously. She didn't treat anyone else that way. Suddenly she felt the urge to tell Moritz that she had stolen a twenty euro bill from the principal's office, and she told him.

"Do you have a guilty conscience?" he asked.

"Yes I do," she said, "very much." But she didn't. She didn't have a bad conscience. He and his friends had tried to break into a cigarette machine and she had taken twenty euros from the principal's office. He and his friends had failed. But not her. She was worse. And assuming it was Frau Petri's coat, then it was really a rotten thing to do. Because Frau Petri especially liked her. Nevertheless, she didn't have a guilty conscience.

"Just give it back tomorrow," he said. "Just put a bill on the desk."

"I don't have one."

"We can scare one up somewhere," he said.

After class Frau Petri told Madalyn she would very much like her to come to Weimar with her ninth grade class. There were three extra spaces for students from other classes. She was definitely going to reserve one for Madalyn. She also apologized for mentioning it to her so late. If Madalyn wanted her to, she'd be happy to talk to her parents about it. Madalyn gave her her mother's cell phone number.

It took her a while to realize that if this came off, she would be spending a week – a whole week! – with Moritz. But also with Claudia.

Chapter Twenty

By the time Madalyn got home Frau Petri had already called up. Her mother wasn't against her going. Quite the opposite. After lunch she sat down at the computer with Madalyn and they searched for pictures of Weimar, descending from outer space into the city via Google Earth and surfing through Wikipedia and other websites for information – which Madalyn soon got tired of.

"Can I go or not?" was all she said.

"Shall I scratch your back?" her mother asked. She burped quietly and pretended to be startled. She wanted to keep Madalyn in suspense and that annoyed her daughter so much she felt like screaming. She knew what was coming; she bet it was a story from her childhood, some beautiful little thing full of meaning, something "magical," always the same. She must not have all that many unscathed memories. It would be some lesson about truth, and would strain to be clever – some example of when she herself had been looking forward to something so much and how "magical" it had been to hope and fear, and that hope and fear were the best part of any happiness, or some stuff like that, which was guaranteed to end with her announcing that the decision for or against Weimar was up to Madalyn, completely up to her – blackmail in short, that would reveal itself in every detail of sentences such as "You've got to decide for yourself if you . . ." or "Do you really think it makes sense for you to . . ." right up to the last minute before departure.

"No," said Madalyn, "I don't want you to scratch my back," and she went to her room.

After a while, her mother knocked on the door, more of a scratchy drumming then a knock. "I think," she said, "you still haven't forgiven me. Sometime or other, you really should, Madi. It could well be that eventually, I won't care anymore. Having children is a kind of depression. Ha, ha . . ."

Madalyn was not up to her mother's witticisms, not to mention the treacly smile her meanness came wrapped in. But at least she had a strategy against her mother's attacks. She wasn't going to play along anymore. She would retreat. She would let Mama and Claudia think they had defeated her, but she would rob them of the fruits of victory. She would give up before either of them could even strike. That would be how to do it. She sat down at her desk, which was a child's desk; around its edge was a frieze of comical. chubby animals in basic colors, pecking at the ground. She wasn't sad or desperate, wasn't filled with hopes and fears. She was in a bad mood. And tired. She could hardly lift her hand because she had no good reason to lift it. She needed to go to the bathroom, but holding her stream seemed the most interesting thing that life had to offer her at the moment. She laid her head on the desk and licked its lacquered wood surface, repeating over and over in a whisper, "Galileo Galilei, Galileo Galilei . . ." Her tongue tripped across her gums like a rubbery comic book figure but she was not longer able to cheer herself up that way. She got even more annoyed at herself just for trying, as if she was still eight years old and had just discovered the great scientist's name – at the time she thought it was the name of a clown. Her breath smelled like chocolate. When they were sitting in front of the computer she had shoveled it into her mouth without thinking, an entire bar gone in a flash. Her mother didn't like milk chocolate and she liked the kind with hazelnuts or pistachios best. I'm going to get fat and comical like a sticker on a child's desk, she thought. So what! She had no trouble imagining Claudia. That goddess of beauty was half a head taller than Madalyn and even if she had been fatter, she would look slimmer. That was also due to her long legs and long arms and long neck. Gymnasts are not fat and they don't get fat either, even if they gorge on chocolate. What did she look like without makeup? And what was her hair like when it wasn't colored? The fact that Moritz lied to Claudia and told her, Madalyn, the truth could just as well mean something not so favorable, namely: being in love with Claudia and not in love with Madalyn. He'd said it was the other way around. However, if you say the truth, it means you have nothing to fear; when you lie, you do. What if we're both in Weimar, Claudia and I? Who will he lie to, her or me? She didn't want to go to Weimar. He'll look at her, she'll look at him – she wouldn't be able to put up with a single glance between the two of them. She was ready to give up. People lie because they want to draw a better picture of themselves, when they fear that the way they are isn't good enough. But he thinks the way he is is good enough for me?

She could hear her mother making a big show of getting her things ready to go to the gym in front of the door to Madalyn's room and she could tell by the sounds how high the level of her mother's anger had risen; and for the first time she thought, She **is** crazy, crazy, crazy. No normal mother goes four or five or sometimes six times a week to the John Harris Gym on Margaretenplatz to lift weights, strap herself into machines to pull, stretch, and heave, punch the man-sized heavy bag, march on a treadmill, pedal a stationary bike, and swim back and forth and back and forth in a twenty-five meter pool for two hours – and why? – so she can look "energetic and businesslike," as she had once described it to her daughter.

I hope she takes off soon, thought Madalyn, and I hope she doesn't come into my room again before she leaves.

Chapter Twenty-One

Moritz said he wanted to have a long talk. "Are you alone?"

"Yes."

"Me too."

She should put her buds in her ears. It was easier, and he would too. She asked if she could call him back in a minute. She had to look for her earbuds and untangle the cable. Why didn't she set her cell phone on speaker, he said. It wouldn't cost anything because he had called her up and not the other way around. He wanted to listen to her moving around her room. It would be like he was there with her. She liked that, and her mood improved right away. She made noises on purpose and talked to herself so he wouldn't just hear nothing at the other end. She described her room to him, made it bigger and described it as more interesting than it was. She didn't think he'd ever get to see it. Suddenly she felt a tender regard for the objects here. She lay down on her bed, pulled up the blanket, put the buds in her ears, and left just a tiny hole to breathe through. He would do the same, he said. First they talked about school, friends, acquaintances, math. Madalyn didn't tell him about Frau Petri inviting her to go to Weimar with his class.

And then Moritz talked about his mother.

"You're the first and only person I've ever told about her," he said.

He was eleven when his mother moved out. Before that there had been such a big fight between his parents he thought that nothing in his life would ever be good again. His father had screamed so loud that a blood vessel in his lung burst and he spit up blood. His mother had a boyfriend and his father had found out. Moritz had already known all about it for a long time. One evening he'd caught the two of them making out in a car parked next to Haydn Park. He had pressed his face against the windshield so no one could try to lie their way out of it. His mother confessed everything and begged him not to tell his father. And he promised he wouldn't. He got to know his mother's boyfriend and thought he was nice and completely normal. Her boyfriend did crazy things with him and gave him puzzle books and other stuff and played a game with him that was called Bad People. You were allowed to say everything you normally weren't allowed to say and think of nasty things to do, like for example taking a nail and scratching it along the side of a big fat Mercedes from the hood to the trunk. His father had always suspected something, and was always very suspicious. So his mother and her boyfriend said that without being asked, Moritz should volunteer the information that he'd been walking around all afternoon in Schönbrunn with his mother and they had played frisbee and had an ice cream by the Gloriette. He should do his best to make it sound believable. He was good at that. And he liked doing it. At the next opportunity he asked if he could think up a story of his own. And the time after that too. His stories became more and more elaborate. Because he had discovered that the more complicated a story was, the more believable it was since everybody thinks you could never make up something like that. For example, that they had seen a man wearing a leather cap on his head and a falcon had been sitting on top of the cap, but the man acted like everything was completely normal. Whoever heard of such a thing? But if that's true, then everything else he said must be true too. The next day his mother told her boyfriend the great story Moritz had served up for his father again and the boyfriend praised him. The three of them were conspirators; but actually they weren't, because Moritz felt sorry for his father – although he had it coming because he was often mean to him – and he had a guilty conscience, too. One day, out of a sense of fairness, he dropped a hint to his father. His father gave him a slap, went and got his mother, and said he should immediately repeat what he had told him. He wouldn't do it so his father had repeated it. In a flash his mother invented a reason why Moritz was angry at her and in his anger had thought up such a nasty thing. Her story was so good that his father believed her. And it was good because his mother had learned from Moritz. The next time she was alone with him, she really gave him hell. He denied everything. He claimed that his father had lied and just said something that he, Moritz, was supposed to have hinted at. His father had invented it and had simply been too much of a coward to say what he wanted to say himself and had therefore claimed that Moritz said it. Moritz's mother believed him. Her boyfriend believed him too. The boyfriend said the father must have become suspicious somehow, and he told Moritz to find out what his father knew, or guessed, or suspected. But Moritz didn't dare ask his father. How could he have without his father thinking that he was again dropping some mendacious hint? On the other hand, he realized that his mother's boyfriend – and before long his mother too – were beginning to suspect him, and he had a bad conscience about them to. He felt like a traitor and he was a traitor. Besides, he had really enjoyed himself on the afternoons he spent with the two of them, because whenever they came back, they sat down with him in the kitchen or invited him to a pastry shop, and the boyfriend always brought Moritz some really neat surprise. His mother was proud of her boyfriend and she kissed him quite openly in front of Moritz. She also liked to kiss her husband in front of Moritz. His father was not sure if Moritz had really lied with his hint or if he had told the truth and his wife had lied. He sat his son down and questioned him closely. In the end he ordered him to keep his eyes and ears open and to tell him right away if he saw or heard anything. His father absolutely had to find out what was up, absolutely. Until he did, he wouldn't be satisfied. And so Moritz now invented a story for him. In it, his mother had a boyfriend, but it was a different boyfriend than her real boyfriend and she met him under different circumstances than the real ones. He invented an affair for his mother with a man who didn't exist so as not to betray her real affair with her boyfriend. And that's what had caused the terrible fight and his mother had moved out. She told Moritz she never wanted to see him again, ever. And she never had seen him again from that day to this. And Moritz's father was also angry with him. Because he would rather have never known anything about it in the first place. He blamed his son that everything was kaput. That's why he had sent him to stay with his sister who lived on the third floor of Number 4 Stuwerstrasse, with the colorful curtains and the Venetian blinds.

When her mother came home from the gym, Madalyn ran out, gave her a hug, and asked her to forgive her. She said she was so sorry that she'd been in a bad mood because a classmate had teased her in front of the whole class and then she'd taken it out on her mother – she decided it would be better not to mention Weimar. She said she'd been unfair and selfish and asked her mother not to be angry with her anymore. She had no trouble turning on the tears. Her mother also started to cry, real tears. She hugged Madalyn close and also asked for forgiveness. She said it was certainly terrible the way the two of them sometimes fought, but in reality they had a wonderful mother-daughter relationship. She knew a lot of people who never fought but had miserable relationships. The way it was between them was much better, didn't Madalyn think so? Yes, said Madalyn, she agreed, but she was thinking of something entirely different.

This classmate had been so nasty to her, she said.

"Who, Bea Haintz?" her mother asked.

"Yeah, Bea," Madalyn lied. "She gets on me whenever she can. Sophie Herbert is having a birthday party today. I think you know her, right? I'm pretty good friends with her. She's quiet but really nice. I like her a lot and she definitely wants me to come. She told me she wished she could celebrate her birthday just with me, but she can't because she'd already invited all her friends before we got to know each other. She invited Bea too and now Bea is jealous of me and was so nasty to me, you can't even imagine how nasty. Now I don't want to go. Sophie called me up three times already, she wants me to come so much. She said she would uninvite Bea if I wanted her to. But I don't."

Her mother said Madalyn should absolutely go to the birthday party. "When does it start?"

Madalyn guessed that behind this question was the unspoken one, When are you coming home?

So she said, "It starts at six."

"Will you be home by ten?" her mother asked.

"Easily," said Madalyn.

Her mother took Madlyn's face between her hands. "By eleven at the latest?" And she nibbled on Madalyn's nose.

Chapter Twenty-Two

She put on her pretty Swedish Angora jacket with horizontal stripes in the seven colors of the rainbow that bled into each other because of the long fibers, and over that her winter coat. She said that Sophie Herbert had told her they were going to shoot off some fireworks from their garden. From their garden in the middle of town? her mother asked. Where were they going to hold the party? Madalyn didn't even know where Sophie Herbert lived. She mumbled that she must have misunderstood and asked why her mother had to be so suspicious right away and was out the door.

She had agreed to meet Moritz at eight o'clock. She took the U4 to Schwedenplatz and continued on the U1 to the Old Danube. She walked across the bridge and along the water, forcing herself to walk at a medium speed when she would have liked to run. She felt hemmed in and alienated from the world and as if she wouldn't have enough strength to fill up the next two hours with thought and movement. She felt like just letting herself fall to the ground. And what if he found her like that and would think she was having a crisis? Everything would be truth between them. She thought she didn't know the value of anything at all, not of love, of loyalty, of truth, justice, or freedom. Up to now she hadn't thought very much about these things, and whenever she heard someone talking about them – her English teacher sometimes did, but in a different language – then she didn't participate in the discussion and took a vacation inside her head, since it was never about the substance but only about the words. She had never met anyone like Moritz and she thought she never would meet anyone like him again in her whole life. *He* lived in those great concepts, at least in some of them. Whether *she* told the truth or not made no difference, at least it hadn't so far. With him, the choice between truth and a lie was a choice between love and hate, almost between life and death. Even with all her mother's moods, she knew that she was loved; and even if she couldn't see an eighth of an inch into her father's brain, it was clear she was his favorite and that, if it came to a choice between his wife and his daughter, he would be on his daughter's side. And hate? What is hate? A bad mood isn't hate and anger isn't hate either, and when you get stubborn and refuse to talk for a day or two, not even that is the least bit like hate. But when a mother runs away and leaves her son behind and never wants to see him again, not at Christmas time and not on his birthday, doesn't call, doesn't send an e-mail, not even a text message, you have to call that hate. And when a father pawns off his son because he can't look him in the eye, what else would a person call that? I have to keep him warm in my arms as long as it takes for everything to be good again, she thought, and what if it takes a lifetime? She got goosebumps on her cheeks, something she'd never felt before.

Now she was walking fast again, hurrying past the house of happiness or disaster, hunching her shoulders and pulling her head in, as if on its interior walls was written what was about to happen there. But that was all just imagination in the head of a certain Madalyn Reis. The windows were dust-covered and nailed shut with boards and didn't look like eyes, which windows in other buildings sometimes did. No secrets. The weathered turquoise didn't seem a bit to her like something lost or abandoned. On the contrary, it was the freakiest and most cheerful house on the road and if she had a lot of money and could choose her own house, she would take this one above all others. But if somebody is desperate, like Moritz was, she thought, cheerfulness in person would probably appear sad to them, and turquoise would seem the color of mourning. Or, it had not been at all the way he told it. At least, she couldn't imagine riding past and thinking, This house is like me. But she would have liked to be somebody who thought that way. I'm just nothing special, she thought again. Did Moritz think about love, loyalty, and truth? Did he discuss them with his friends? Or with Claudia? Please not with Claudia, she thought and pressed her fists against her mouth. His telephone voice was different than when he was right there with her: more calm, more adult, but more brutal too; sometimes at the end of a sentence it sank to a hoarse bass – because of the cigarettes? – which she actually liked. She mustn't interrupt the moment of silence that followed, otherwise the little dreams that fluttered up in it couldn't be grasped. Sometimes there had been big dreams among them: that they would go away together, for example, Madalyn and Moritz, Moritz and Madalyn, to a country whose language they couldn't understand, to a city in Africa for example, where no one was concerned with formalities, and that would be the beginning of everything they could become, and they really would be able to become something. She had often spun out such dreams in the empty afternoons or in the evening before going to bed, or in school. It was because of such dreams that she loved geography class and the voice of Herr Lunzer and the way he ran his fingertips under his glasses and rubbed his eyes. Until now she had always imagined herself alone in those foreign lands and cities, shod in sturdy hiking boots and wearing indestructible jeans and carrying nothing but a rucksack, her sunglasses shoved up on her head and Dextropur tablets in her jeans pocket. At home with the help of Google Street View she had hopped around London and New York, Madrid and Lisbon, and had looked at Lagos and Cape Town, Istanbul and Kuala Lumpur from the air, but also at the beaches of Panama, the mouth of the Amazon, and the course of the Congo. She could clearly imagine living with Moritz in a little apartment in some tropical country with voices and honking outside, red Venetian blinds like the ones in his room through which the sun shone, throwing bands of shadow onto the kitchen table where they sat eating something spicy and discussing the day to come. He had suffered so much abuse. He thinks he has no one. She would bet that neither his father nor his mother nor his mother's boyfriend had a guilty conscience. He had lied because he was afraid they wouldn't like him anymore if he told the truth, and now he thinks he has to keep lying, lying all the time, and never dare to say what's really going on inside him. But he can tell me, she thought. I will always love him and the more honest he is with me, the more I will love him. However, she feared – and had no defense against it; it was like too much Tabasco – he might have told her his sad story only to soften her up, to prepare her for something else. She had lost her compass, didn't know if she should be glad that he had confided in her or afraid of another confession – every confession a new truth that the next confession turned into a lie. She was very sure that something important would happen tonight.

It had warmed up that afternoon and a warm wind was still blowing. The smell of spring rose from the water, a smell of straw and beach and impregnated wood. She took off her coat and carried it under her arm. Pedestrians approached her from the opposite direction and men in their undershirts were already working in the gardens in front of some of the weekend cottages. Next to the boat houses men were painting little boats red, blue, yellow, and white. She could only see the water from a few places because most of the shoreline and docks were private, with hedges growing in front of them or mats of woven reeds, taller than a man, lashed to their fences. She came to a small park where there were wooden tables and benches shaded by a widespreading tree. She sat down on a bench next to the water and looked over at the skyscrapers of the UN-City against the pale evening sky. She draped the coat over her shoulders and put up the collar in order to be more to herself. Seagulls and swallows flew past and her eyes flitted after the swallows' lightning maneuvers. A set of concrete steps led down into the water, where they were covered with a pelt of algae. She kept taking her cell phone out of her pocket to look at the screen and see what time it was. In the summer, she and her parents sometimes took the subway as far as Kaisermühlen. They would take their bikes along, bring something to eat and a blanket, and ride three abreast along the path that led, straight as an arrow, from one end of the Danube Island to the other and back. She entertained them by doing tricks on her little bike while making faces. Her father imitated her. She had to get off her bike she was laughing so hard and her mother took pictures.

She strolled downstream a little. Here it smelled of french fries. There was a café in one of the boat houses. She was hungry. She wouldn't be able to keep anything down anyway. At least, not until Moritz was there. Besides, she had no money, not a cent. She would take a hundred big steps and then turn around. Suddenly she was no longer sure it wouldn't be better after all to have slightly longer hair. Moritz had said it would always grow back. For sure she didn't want the fright wig she used to have. It wouldn't be bad to color her hair, either. Black would look especially good. But she wouldn't be allowed to, no, never.

At last she got back to the house. There was a conifer in the front garden that was taller than all the other trees in the neighborhood. And there was a palm tree, a short one, with a trunk like a giant gray wooden pineapple. Next to it stood a cement figure missing its head. It was holding a spear and shield and had a sword at its belt and a short skirt like a Roman soldier. She hadn't noticed any of this the last time she was here. And the fence seemed higher, too. And there were a lot more people on the path, cyclists, walkers, and joggers. In the gathering darkness the house no longer looked friendly. With a little imagination, it was easy to see that it had once been friendly; now it was gloomy and tumbledown. Maybe Moritz had discovered it in the evening or on a rainy day. Probably. In a quarter of an hour it would be eight. She felt her heart pounding.

She saw him. Saw him from far away. He was running. He was hurrying. She stood by the hedge across from the entrance. He couldn't see her. He was a good five minutes too early. According to her cell phone, seven minutes. But still, he was hurrying. That made her happy. It swept the worry from her head. She stepped out of the shadows and without a word he embraced her. That's what she had hoped for. She had to stand on tiptoe to reach his mouth and he had to bend down to reach hers. His big hands rested on her back. They'll be cold, she thought, and took them under her coat and clamped them in her armpits.

"Quick," he whispered, "now's a good time."

No one was to be seen on the path. A little light was left in the sky. Moritz lifted Madalyn up until she could grab hold of the top rail. She was over in a second. And he was right behind her. Madalyn ran ahead, ran around the house, and stood in the niche next to the back door. Moritz reached through the window, and they were inside.

Chapter Twenty-Three

Inside it was pitch black. Moritz had brought his rucksack along.

He asked Madalyn to hold the cigarette lighter up so he could see to unpack it. He had taken two cups of fruit yogurt from his aunt's refrigerator, raspberry and cherry, and had two spoons as well. He took out two cheese sandwiches and two sausage sandwiches he had made himself, a slice of tomato to go with them and a dill pickle with the sausage, all of it wrapped in aluminum foil, plus paper napkins. He had also brought a fresh pack of yellow Parisienne cigarettes and four small bottles of beer – Corona, the best kind. He said his aunt's boyfriend drank only Corona. It was Mexican, lighter than Ottakringer or Zipfer. Especially for Madalyn. He had gotten the four bottles as a present, officially.

"Is all the beer in your cache gone?" asked Madalyn.

And he'd also thought of candles.

They let some hot wax drip onto the stairs, pressed the candle ends into it, sat down on the stairs, and were surrounded by a circle of flickering light, as if they were the object of a conspiracy.

Moritz couldn't get enough kissing and hugging. He kept saying something, again and again. But she couldn't understand what it was. Didn't want to ask. It wouldn't have been appropriate. Although she would have liked to know. It was always the same thing he said and it probably had some special significance. Or maybe not. He smelled good. He said he'd shaved just for Madalyn. He held the back of her head with his hand. That was beautiful.

When they had eaten and shared a beer, they didn't know what more to say for a while. Maybe because Madalyn had asked about his cache of beer.

"I know what you're thinking," he said at last.

"No you don't," she said. "There's no way you can know. Did you sleep with Claudia?" And before he could answer, she made the question more precise: "Did you sleep with Claudia in this house?"

There was flickering candlelight around them, but still she could see very well from his face that he was getting ready to lie. And he must have seen in her face that she wouldn't believe him, not this time.

"Yeah, I did," he said.

"But not today, right?"

"Today? Of course not!"

She had to cry and couldn't do it quietly. She pulled out of his arms, ran down the few steps to the floor and over to a window. She held her hands in front of her face and bent forward because her stomach was cramping.

"And yesterday I was here at night with a couple friends, I admit it, and we drank all the beer. That's why there's none left. I lied to you. I'm sorry, Madalyn. Afterwards we went to the Flex. Sorry." And he repeated, "I know exactly what you're thinking."

And she repeated, "There's no way you can know what I'm thinking!"

He came down and stood right behind her. He didn't dare touch her. Kept saying her name, at the end without any inflection. And wanted to tell her something again. But she wouldn't have been able to take it.

"You're just lying again," she said, her voice much too high. "Why do you always lie? Why? I don't believe anything you say anymore. I can't believe you anymore, Moritz. You never would have had to lie to me. You just lie because you lie. Why do you do that?"

He returned to the stairs, but first he circled the room, his hands in his pockets; dragged his feet across the floor. She watched him from the side.

"Come to me," he said.

He sat down on the stairs and put his head in his hands. His shoulders were trembling a little. But she didn't believe him.

"I'm not with her anymore," he said. "I swear I'm not. We met up today, that's true. After school – at noon, I mean. I can't tell you exactly where we met. She called me up. She told me you had talked to her. We met down on Mariahilferstrasse, there's some kind of computer store there, a new one I think. She wanted to go there because she's getting a new computer. Her parents just give her one when she wants it. She asked me if I would take a look at it with her, but I didn't want to because I don't know anything about computers, and I didn't want to anyway."

She knew what he was doing. She was familiar with this trick. You tell something that's unimportant and that everybody believes and you attach your lie to that; and because everybody believes the first thing, they believe the lie too.

"I'm not going to sleep with you," she said.

"I never thought you would," he said.

His voice dropped down into the bass range, and because it was dark and she now turned her back to him again, he sounded like he did on the telephone, and she waited for something to happen to her.

"In that case, in that case I'd better leave now," he said. "I can't change anything at this point anyway. You don't believe me, and I can understand why."

He stood up. She heard him descending the steps. She waited. Hoped he would come over to her again. Hoped he would touch her this time, put his arms around her.

"It's best for us to leave together," he said. "It's not good to be alone here in this house. I don't think you want to stay here alone, do you? Let's put the candles out and leave. I'll take you to the subway. Or you can leave by yourself right away, once we get outside. Up to you."

He came to her. She turned to him and saw that his lower lip was trembling. Now she believed him.

"You just didn't know me before," she said.

"Exactly," he said.

She was crying again, but not so hard. He took her hand and drew her back into the circle of light. He lit a cigarette and asked if she wanted one too.

"Just a drag from yours," she said and sat down on the step above him.

"Shit," he said.

"Please don't say that you always mess everything up, please," she said.

"That's exactly what I was going to say," he said.

He looked at her briefly with a strange, pleading expression that confused her because she couldn't evaluate it: if he meant it seriously, it was pathetic and wouldn't get him anywhere; if it was pretend, i.e. another lie, it might touch her because it was so obviously helpless, as if he had finally reached the end of his lies. She remembered during their very first telephone conversation how she had wished she could cradle him in her arm and he could cry, because she had thought she was the only one he wouldn't need to be ashamed with. I only have to bend down to him and take his head into my lap, she thought, and say his name again and again just like he said mine again and again a little while ago. I'll accept anything he tells me. She was aware that there was some movie romance in her thoughts but that felt good. Whatever I experience, they could make a film about it. That felt good.

He stretched one leg out, fished in his pocket, and pulled out a twenty-euro bill. "I promised I'd get you one."

At first she didn't know what he meant. She was a thief. She accused him of being a liar, and she was a thief.

"You wanted to give the money back," he said. "Just put it on the table in the conference room. That's how I'd do it. You only borrowed it. I'll give you an extra euro interest and you can add that to it so everybody knows that it was just borrowed. That's how I'd do it."

"And where'd you get the money?"

"It's mine."

"I don't believe that. You took it from somewhere too."

"Yeah, I stole it just like you."

"Who'd you steal it from?"

"From my aunt."

"Then I don't want it."

He boosted himself up a step and sat right next to her, pressing his face into the angora wool of her jacket. He can't have even noticed the jacket, she thought, it's too dark here. But he knows it's soft.

"I promised I'd get it for you," he said. "I may be a liar, but I keep my promises." She stroked his hair and his ear. "I just borrowed it too. You can give it back to me sometime and I'll return it to my aunt. I took it for you. It doesn't matter a bit. She's so messy she won't even notice. It was for us, because we telephoned with each other. I'll give it back to her some time. Just take it."

Thief, liar, liar, thief – it didn't matter, it was all the two of them together. And anyway, how would they live in Africa, for example, if not exactly like this – as liars and thieves? No one must know what was up with them. Money had the effect of making her feel better. That's obvious, she thought. Money was even better than a bit of movie romance. She put the bill in her pocket, imitating the way he had stretched out one leg and reached into the pocket of his jeans.

"Or you won't give it back," he said. "Up to you."

Chapter Twenty-Four

They didn't stay in the house that evening. Madalyn didn't want to. Nor did she want Moritz to kiss her anymore. At least not in that house. When he put his arms around her and rubbed his face against hers, she ducked into the clinch like a boxer protecting himself against blows. She said she never wanted to enter this house again. Everything in it reminded him of Claudia anyway. He said that wasn't so. On the bridge over the Old Danube she kissed him. In the middle of the bridge, on purpose. Nevertheless, not everything was good inside her.

Moritz wanted to introduce her to his friends, at least some of them. He had a lot, a whole lot of friends, cool guys. It might not be obvious right away, but every single one was a cool guy. She didn't believe him, but said nothing. Everything about him was lonely. The way he sat in the subway was lonely. To say nothing of his mouth. The way his voice sometimes dropped at the end of the sentence was lonely. His jacket, not least because he always wore the same one. She asked if he would go shopping for a jacket with her, preferably where he had bought his. The way he nodded, with his eyes half closed, was lonely. His cold hands that were not beautiful, but reddened and pale. He wants to be lonely; he doesn't want to be lonely. Wants to be, doesn't want to be. She didn't believe he had any friends. Or if he did, not good ones.

She got drunk in the Flex. And threw up. Was ashamed. When she talked, she listened to her own voice again. There were some guys there and Moritz said they were his friends. What had they been like? Two, three, four, – she told me she couldn't remember how many. She had gotten tipsy. Why? Because everybody was standing around with a bottle of beer in their hand. Had the others been drunk too? Most of them. What about Moritz? He wasn't. Had he told her she shouldn't drink so much? Yeah, that's exactly what he said. And why had she done it anyway? She couldn't remember how much she had drunk. Even a little made her sick. In there it was loud, all techno, which she hated. And it was stifling and dirty and the bathroom was a total pigsty. Most of the time they sat outside on the benches by the Danube Canal. She threw up into the water while Moritz watched. He didn't pretend like she wasn't with him. No, that's not how he acted. But he didn't hold her while she was doing it. He saw she was feeling miserable but he hadn't held her. She probably wouldn't have wanted him to anyway. She didn't know what she would have wanted. He stood in the path with his hands balled up in his pockets and his legs apart and watched her as she hung over the railing. She felt like she had ruined her life. Like nothing would become of her now. Not as long as she lived. She would never be able to begin again. She would completely mess up the math test. It was already way past eleven. She had made such a mess of her life. She had never kept her good resolutions. She would never be a regular customer in Frau Jeller's bookstore. Her eyes flitted the way they had flitted after the swallows. She couldn't really see clearly. And then she drank something pink and sweet. She kept it down. But she had to be careful not to collapse. Moritz asked if he should take her home. She didn't want him to. Because she thought he didn't really want to. He didn't ask a second time. She wanted to go alone. And she did. She went alone, thinking that when she was done walking, her life would be over.

At some point there was some guy beside her. It was possible he had been beside her the whole time. She had no idea. He was all dressed in black. She didn't know him. He was saying nice things. He said he knew her. And explained how. But she didn't listen. She couldn't, because she was too busy breathing carefully. Nevertheless, she learned something from him: the house – the empty one with a boarded-up windows down by the Old Danube –

belonged to the boyfriend of Moritz's aunt. Didn't she know that? Yeah, yeah, she knew that, of course she did. He called him Moritz, not Rizzo. Nobody in the Flex had called him Rizzo. The guy walking next to her gave her a cigarette. She kept it in her hand, but didn't take a drag. The house was going to be torn down that summer. Until then, they were allowed to do what they wanted in it. She asked him the name of Moritz's girlfriend. She was his girlfriend, he said. Was he sure? As far as he knew, at least. And suddenly he was gone, the nice guy, and she was sitting in the U4. She got out at Kettenbrückengasse. Her legs were so heavy that the way up the stairs had never seemed so far.

And when she got home, all hell broke loose.

It was 12:30. She was drunk. Her beautiful jacket that could only be washed in cold water was splattered with throw-up. Her parents stared at her as if she had horns on her head. Her father held both hands over his nose and mouth. She couldn't defend herself because she knew very well there was no defense. And besides, her tongue was heavy. She stank of beer and the sweet pink stuff and cigarettes and vomit. Her mother started in by saying they would take her out of school. She had given up having any expectations of Madalyn. She'd lost all hope. All joy. All pride. All her mother's happiness. What she had said that noon about their wonderful mother-daughter relationship was a joke and had always been a joke. During the last two hours, thank God she had finally been able to neutralize in her heart that thing called her daughter. Not that it had been hard. No, it had been easy. It had been long overdue. They'd see if they could find something for her. Because she wouldn't be able to do it herself. Unfortunately, it wouldn't be possible to convince anyone that she was good for anything. That would be a lie. And someone else in the family was in charge of lying. Might she have any interest in the retail grocery trade? At least that would be economically secure – people always needed to eat. Maybe there was a job for her at Hofer or at Billa on the Rechte Wienzeile, at least for a week or two. No one would keep her much longer than that in any case, because they would soon see through her. With luck she could work as a cashier but otherwise she could stock shelves. But her mother could tell her one thing for certain: they would make sure the job was here in the neighborhood so everyone could see what she had made of herself. Then all this shit would at least have some point. Then she could play the honorable role of cautionary example. She was absolutely serious. Better a cautionary example than a pile of shit that's just an embarrassment to everybody and not even good for exercising one's sympathy on – there were enough Gypsies in town for that and they deserved it more. Oh and by the way, something that went without saying but possibly had not made a landing in her little drunken brain yet: she could crumple up Weimar and stick it wherever she wanted. She would never get there in her life. What would a stupid shelf-stocker do in the town of German classicism, anyway? If she was lucky, really really lucky and took very very much vitamin B, she might make it as the copy machine bimbo in some office. But the world would have to cut her a whole lot of slack for that to ever happen.

Her father didn't say a word. Madalyn didn't care what his face looked like while he listened.

Before she got into bed she looked to see if there was a text message from Moritz. There wasn't. But when she woke up in the morning, there were ten. And in all of them, he talked about love. And the later he had sent them, the longer they were. And they contained no mistakes, which could only mean that he was not drunk when he wrote them. The last text message had been sent at 4 AM. In it, he wrote that she was making him a better person and that he'd never met anyone like her and that he wanted to stay with her as long as he lived and that they could always begin again somewhere new.

    She replied in the same vein.

Chapter Twenty-Five

I stayed at our table in Neni's for a while. In my breast was a chunk of cement that was of no use to anyone hoping for a foundation on which to build. I felt helpless. Here's what I felt like doing at once: going back to the Heumühlgasse, pounding on the door of the apartment directly below mine, and at last giving the lovely Frau Reis a piece of my mind, one she would never forget for the rest of her life. I intended to tot up Madalyn's life for her, starting with the day she was hit by a car in front of our building and would probably have cried for her mother except that by the time she was five years old, she already knew that her crying wouldn't be heard because instead of doing her maternal duty, her mother preferred to get in her workout at the John Harris Gym on Margaretenplatz so she could be or stay or become "energetic and businesslike," which in the end was to be endorsed when you considered the damage aggression might do if it wasn't worked off daily on the free weights, the heavy bag, the treadmill and the fitness machines. I closed my eyes and a wave of imageless violence washed through *my* brain, causing a flush that made me take a few deep breaths before I could think clearly again.

When I suggested that she should ask Moritz if he would forgo the trip to Weimar, Madalyn had looked directly at me and smiled, and a bitter – a very grown-up and bitter expression had appeared on her face. It was I who had estimated too highly the feelings of the guy she loved so much – and not highly enough her capacity for suffering. She didn't answer. It was as if we had exchanged places. I – still wet behind the ears, naïve, idealistic; she – mild, forbearing, without illusions, mature, and with no memory of the child. I should have summoned up all my strength, imagination, intelligence, charm, and disingenuousness and – despite a reluctance bordering on disgust and my conviction (but what is a conviction anyway, especially a "professional" one!) – talked to her mother after all. Even if it meant that her No would be even more adamant; no means no, whether hard or soft. It would have shown Madalyn that I was ready to assume part of the failure.

She thanked me for the meal and left the restaurant without another word. She paused briefly in the passageway of the Naschmarkt, looked around as if she was waiting for someone (I watched her through the glass door), dug her hands into her jeans pockets, hunched her shoulders, and disappeared between the fruit stands.

I was the one who had saved her life. That had to impose an obligation, didn't it? I had never considered myself responsible for truth. Why would I start now? I had to face the fact that I had missed my chance; without knowing how that chance might have looked.

I paid the check and walked through the Naschmarkt and over to Karlsplatz. The museum where Evelyn works is right next to the Karlskirche, and it was improbable that I wouldn't find her there. We hadn't seen each other for a month and had spoken only once on the telephone. I hadn't been in the museum for two years. I didn't know what she would make of my visit. She liked Madalyn and had often asked after her. I wasn't there to ask her advice but to be comforted.

We sat in the cafeteria in the glassed-over inner courtyard of the museum. Evelyn looked tired and had on something black and tight-fitting. She chewed on her lower lip and looked at me with her hooded eyes.

"What's up?" she asked.

"Will you come to my place again sometime?" I asked.

"Or you come to mine," she answered matter-of-factly.

"I meant to call you up," I said. "But I would much rather look at you when we talk to each other."

"That's nice," she said. "Very nice. I'll come tonight if you like."

She talked about her work and I talked about mine. I said nothing about Madalyn.

From the beginning, I had resisted defining us as a couple. "What are we?" she once asked. "Two people who get together fairly often," I had answered. She stuck out her tongue and showed me her backside. A year and a half ago, we separated. Whatever that may mean. In any event, it didn't mean that we stopped seeing each other from time to time or stopped phoning each other – sometimes talking for a long time, although she lived no more than two hundred yards away as the crow flies. Nor did it mean that I didn't spend the night at her place from time to time, or she at mine. We were a reliable emotional safety valve for each other. Sometimes I went with her when she and colleagues went out to a vineyard restaurant. Afterwards I would be embarrassed because I had acted so unironically. Other times we invited Robert and Hanna to dinner at Cantinetta Antinori, or they invited us – as if everything was the way it had been a year and a half ago.

I had already reached the fountain in front of the Karlskirche when I heard her calling after me. She came running up, her legs kicking out sideways like a schoolgirl's.

"We talked about everything," she cried, "except the most important thing: my exhibit!"

She gave me a copy of the catalog: *Vienna in the Cold War: World Capital of Espionage*. She'd been planning this exhibit for eight years. We'd often discussed it. I promised I'd come to the opening.

"I'm going to Trieste for Holy Week," she said. "Want to come along?"

I said I'd think it over. And I really did intend to. Evening had fallen in the meantime. I was so tired I thought I wouldn't be able to make it the short distance home. I took a taxi. The driver asked if I was from Vienna and said that because of the one-way streets, he'd have to make a pretty big detour to get me to the Heumühlgasse. It wouldn't take me any longer on foot than with the taxi. I said I wanted him to drive me there anyway.

At home, Madalyn was waiting for me. She was sitting on my doorstep.

"He's going to stay here with me," she whispered. "He doesn't want to go to Weimar without me."

She was in heaven, if I may be permitted to use that expression just this once.

Chapter Twenty-Six

I didn't go to Trieste. Evelyn didn't pressure me to. I told her I needed to start writing. Otherwise, my dark hero was threatening to abandon me. He had dominated my days until Madalyn and her story pushed him aside.

Evelyn asked if I would look in on her cat Pnin now and then during Holy Week and water her ferns. She would prefer that I do it instead of one of the women she worked with. Pnin was an old Tiger cat used to being alone most of the time. Whenever we encountered each other, I held my fist in front of her face and she bumped her head against it. When Evelyn and I agreed to end our relationship, I couldn't bring myself to give back the key to her apartment and she must have felt the same way about my key. It would never have occurred to either of us to enter the other's apartment without ringing first. Although Evelyn warned me sarcastically not to confuse it with mutual respect, since it was nothing but a traffic regulation between "two people who meet fairly frequently," I guessed that she was as much in favor of it as I was.

I plunged into my work, read through what I had already written, began a new chapter – more playfully than seriously – slept on the couch, and again felt the excitement that's like a warm wind in winter – what I would ask for if my God were to grant me only one more wish. That's how I spent the first days of Holy Week. I was alone and spoke to no one.

On Wednesday morning Madalyn rang the doorbell.

She quickly shut the door behind her, ducked under my arm without even saying hello, and scampered into the library. She stood next to the spiral stairs that go up to my rooftop study, held the banister with one hand and gave me a stunning smile as if posing for a photograph.

"I came to say thank you," she said.

"I don't believe you," I said.

She widened her eyes and opened her mouth and laughed as if I had told her a super joke and she was being filmed. She said she didn't know anyone as direct and honest as me. I replied that both things were typical of someone my age, and that made her laugh even more. She dropped into the leather armchair where she had sat during our first interview; and now she was suddenly embarrassed.

Could she be honest too? Speak openly with me? Because she had something to ask me. Namely, if she and Moritz could sleep together at my place.

I said I didn't understand. Which wasn't a very bright thing to say.

"Moritz and I want to sleep together." She spoke with exaggerated enunciation. "But we can't do it at his place and for sure not at mine, and I don't want to do it in the house on the Old Danube."

What good to me now was the ordering, shaping power of literature, its ability to make the confusions of life lucid and transparent? Had I not seized every opportunity – in total agreement with Frau Petri – to proclaim that literature was a catalog of precedents meant to comfort us because they show that others before us have already done and suffered what we do and suffer?

"I know what you're thinking," she said, the corners of her mouth twitching mockingly, and then quoted herself. "You're going to say I can't know what you're thinking. But I do. You think that Moritz is the one who wants to, and I just want to because he does. I think you can't stand him. You know why I think that?"

"No, I don't know why."

"You never lie, right?"

I said "Madalyn" and nothing more.

"You don't like him because he always lies, that's clear. But he doesn't lie anymore. He doesn't lie to me. I know he doesn't. He doesn't have to promise not to. I know what's a lie and what isn't a lie. I'm sorry you don't like him; it's my fault you don't. You don't know him and I know him so well." She spoke quickly, waving her hands in front of her face and staring into space as if she was at a casting, reciting a standard role. "Listen, why don't you believe me? If you knew him you'd like him, I'm sure you would. He has so many stories to tell; you could use them in your work. At least, I get so many ideas when I'm with him that I could sit down every night and write a novel. I think I was a dumbhead before I met him, that's exactly what I think, I was a dumbhead. He makes everything magical. Why don't you believe me! I used to think the world was just the path between Heumühlgasse and Rahlgasse and not much else. And now everything is full of magic. But for him it was always like it is for me now, and that's why everybody thought he was lying. I'm so happy, I'm so fantastically happy, really. But then people say it's a lie because they don't understand. Is that what you think? I don't really believe that's what you think, right? I'm so glad you said I should ask him if he'd stay here . . ."

"I don't dislike him," I interrupted her, "but it doesn't matter."

The jacket she was wearing, the blue and white sport jacket she had worn at our interview and also at Neni's – had she bought it with Moritz as she had wanted to? Had she and Moritz gone to the bookstore of my friend Anna Jeller in the meantime and looked for a book together that told a story like theirs? Or had they had a deep discussion about poetry? Or maybe he had in fact begun to write poems? Because she encouraged him. Because in the end it was *she* who "made everything magical." Where did Frau Malic ever get the idea that Herr and Frau Reis belonged to a sect? And if she was right, would Madalyn have told me about it?

And finally I said it: "I can't do it, Madalyn, and I don't want to, either."

She smiled inwardly as if she was thinking something quite different. "Funny, I imagined that's exactly what you would say. You said it once before, word for word, and everything worked out fine anyway. You say no, and then it turns out all right. That's funny. I told Moritz, Guaranteed he'll say no, and then everything will be all right. I told him that's the kind of man you are. It would only be once, one single time, and we wouldn't mess anything up. You wouldn't even know we'd been here. We only want to sleep with each other once. I've never slept with anyone, and Moritz only once before."

"Madalyn," I said, and even I found it idiotic to keep repeating her name. "Madalyn, I don't care. I don't want to know about it. You can insult somebody by telling him things he doesn't want to know."

She folded her hands, pinned them between her knees, continued to look at the ground, and turned calm and very serious. "Funny," she said. "I prepared so carefully for this conversation. I thought out exactly what I would say, and I thought out exactly what you would say."

"Unfortunately, I can't say what you thought I would."

"But you are saying exactly what I thought you would. It's okay. I'm just surprised you're saying exactly what I thought you would. Because usually, it's exactly what I've thought out that doesn't happen."

She stood up, reached her arms above her head and twisted and stretched.

I didn't want to let her leave like this. "I'll make us some hot chocolate," I said, "and you can tell me how you did in math. Did your German teacher read our interview? What'd she think?"

"I know exactly what you're thinking," she said again. "You think Moritz sent me. But he didn't. He doesn't know I'm here."

She was contradicting herself, but who was I to point that out to her? "So what if he does know? My God, I wouldn't care," I said.

I went to the kitchen and poured milk into a pot. I dumped in a couple spoonfuls of cocoa powder and added some vanilla sugar and put it on the stove. She waited in the doorway and watched. I was expecting her to start crying any minute and tried to arm myself against it. But she didn't. She told me she'd been unbelievably lucky on the math test. There were two problems she had prepared for, and exactly those two, down to the same numbers, had been on the test. So she solved those perfectly, and at least she had been on the right track with two other problems. She found that out when she compared notes with the others after class. She was sure she would get at least a C- and maybe even a C. A C- for sure. Frau Eistleitner, the math teacher, said she wasn't going to return the math test until after Easter because she didn't want to spoil anyone's vacation. That sounded awful, as if she had already looked at them and the grades were bad. But she didn't think so; nobody in her class thought so. Frau Eistleitner was very nice and when they had done badly on a test, she was the one who felt the worst. Frau Petri had taken our interview along on the trip to Weimar and promised to read it on the bus. She'd already read one page and liked it very much. – All this was said in a cheerful and easy-going way, as if she had never asked what she had asked a few minutes ago.

We went back to the library. We took a long time to finish our hot chocolate. When our cups were empty she brought them back to the kitchen and said she wouldn't disturb me anymore.

At the door, I asked her to do me a favor. I had to take a trip for a few days, until noon on Easter Sunday to be exact, to do some research for the novel I was working on – perhaps she remembered my mentioning it – and up on the roof outside my study there were some pots with tomato seedlings. They definitely needed to be watered, i.e., they needed a bit of water every day, not much, only a little, and please not on the leaves. Tomatoes didn't like that. Just a little water for the roots would be enough. Could she do that for me? I gave her my extra key. I was planning to leave today, I said, in about two hours. On Sunday, she could simply leave the key on the kitchen table and lock the door behind her. Would she do me that favor?

I spent the following days in Evelyn's apartment, wrote my way through my "smooth time" (Roland Barthes), played with the cat, warmed up what I found in the refrigerator. At night I went to a hotel. A few minutes' walk from Evelyn's apartment there's a place with the interesting name Hotel Pineapple. Supposedly it belongd to a trade union. A colleague of mine told me that. She had put up a desperate character there for a while in one of her novels.

I felt very good. Very. Good.

Chapter Twenty-Seven

For two months I heard nothing more from Madalyn. We ran into each other once in the stairwell. She nodded a silent hello and was glad we were headed in opposite directions. Another time I saw her through the window of Café Sperl. She was on her way to school and we waved to each other. I understood her embarrassment and wasn't angry with her. I didn't see her again until the end of May. It was a day I will never forget, May 26th, a Tuesday.

That morning I had breakfasted at the Sperl with my friend Frau Moser, who owns the furniture store across from the coffeehouse and has a political clarity that I would be happy to get implanted in myself. Like me, she's close to the Social Democrats but unlike me, she doesn't hold back with criticism. I fear losing what little is left of my ideological home if I keep my eyes wide open. I'd already been tempted a couple times to talk to her about Madalyn. I should have done so, because it turned out she had already encountered her, and Moritz too. She told me about it later.

As I left the café, someone said my name. He was standing close to the wall by the entrance. I didn't have the slightest doubt it was Moritz. I recognized him by his mouth and his jacket in the colors of a can of Red Bull. He wanted to talk to me. He extended his hand. A soft pressure. His cheeks were glowing. We walked along side-by-side and he was silent. We walked very quickly. I thought he was going to take me somewhere. Was Madalyn okay, I asked. He nodded. His school backpack hung from one shoulder. He preceded me into the little park with swings and seesaws and climbing structures where eight years ago I had watched Madalyn learn to ride her bike. We sat down on a bench. He smoked. Didn't offer me one.

"What's up with Madalyn?" I asked.

He shook his head and took his time answering. "She wasn't in school today. The police were there and asked if anybody knew anything. She didn't come home last night. Her parents called the police this morning. And they came to school to question her classmates. But nobody knows anything."

I felt the skin of my face turn icy cold.

He kept shaking his head. Almost imperceptibly, as if he had a tic. "I thought you might know where she is."

"How would I know where Madalyn is? I absolutely do not know where Madalyn is."

"I thought she was at your house."

"At my house? Why would she be there!"

He was familiar with my kitchen, my bathroom, my library, and probably my study too, and he knew I was thinking about that at this moment.

"She likes you a lot," was all he said and continued to tremble from his head down into his shoulders.

I told him to tell me everything. Right now. Otherwise I'd take him to see Madalyn's parents, I threatened, without knowing how I would have managed that.

He said he didn't think anything had happened. It was sure to be nothing. What would've happened? But he knew the reason she hadn't gone home last night. He knew exactly why. And again he said that Madalyn really liked me. I did not like him. I wanted to tell him to cut out the stupid trembling, that I didn't buy his idiotic trembling. I was dying to yell at him. Instead, I put my hand on his shoulder. Because I imagined he would tell Madalyn about it and she would say about me, See? That's exactly what he's like, he's exactly like that.

He calmed down.

He said that a few days ago, her parents had given her a big piece of news. Namely, that they were going to move away for two years. Far away. To Hong Kong, in fact. Madalyn's father was going to work there. He wasn't going to work in Hong Kong, actually, but in another city nearby. Moritz didn't know if he'd gotten everything exactly straight; he'd forgotten the name of the town. It was a huge city, with twice as many inhabitants as the whole country of Austria. He'd never heard of this town before. (It was Shenzhen, as I have learned in the meantime. Herr Reis was one of a team of western engineers and managers who had been assigned to develop a site for the production of computer chips in China. The German parent company was taking advantage of the economic crisis to restructure or close factories in Germany, Austria, the Netherlands, and the US, where production costs were too high. A number of especially qualified employees had the possibility – or rather, were confronted with the alternative – of going to China for a certain length of time or be laid off. Herr Reis and his wife had decided on the former.) They were going to live in Hong Kong, Moritz said, because that was a better place for westerners. Hong Kong was like New York without the crime. Madalyn's father would be at work four days a week and only come home on the weekends, but he would be making a fantastic amount of money. An apartment in Hong Kong had already been arranged by the Chinese. They were going to move even before summer vacation began – that meant in June, a little less than a month from now. For the time being they were going to rent out their apartment in Vienna. They didn't know yet what the situation would be in two years. In Hong Kong Madalyn would attend an English private school with the sons and daughters of managers, diplomats, and academics from all over the world. It would be a once-in-a-lifetime opportunity for her. In two years she would speak perfect English and fairly good Chinese and a bit of some other languages, which would stand her in good stead in the future.

Her parents had known about all this for quite some time, by the way. They hadn't told Madalyn because they wanted to surprise her. They really thought it was going to make Madalyn happy.

"She's not happy," I said.

"No," he said, "she's not." He gave me a suspicious look. He didn't like me any more than I liked him. Even if I did put my hand on his shoulder. It wasn't worth my while to make a secret of it. "She hates her parents," he said and exhaled so strongly that it obscured his words and I didn't understand all of them. "Really hates them . . . You wouldn't understand . . ."

"I don't need to understand. When are you finally going to tell me what's up with her?"

"But you can't tell anybody else." He had become soft again.

"What am I not supposed to tell? And not tell who?"

"The police, for instance."

"Why would the police want to talk to me?"

"Madalyn wanted us to run off, the two of us together. She's been wanting that the whole time, but I didn't take her seriously."

They had been fantasizing that they would live together somewhere – anywhere – on earth. Madalyn had thought out exactly what their apartment would look like. A kitchen with a little balcony, for example. She'd even made drawings of it. It had been a game. He'd been a hundred percent certain it was a game for Madalyn too. What else could it be, the way she'd overdone it? You only exaggerate like that when you're not serious. Sometimes they walked through Vienna speaking English to each other and pretending they were in an American city, Chicago or New York, and then their apartment was in Chicago or New York. Or they spoke French and then their apartment was in Paris. Or they had walked along the Danube and pretended it was somewhere in Africa, so the apartment was somewhere in Africa. They had played at being ten years older and a married couple and they would speculate on the stock market and soon become multimillionaires and give away half their money. For example, they would stick €5000 in bills into the cardboard coffee cup of a certain woman who begged on the stairs to the Kettenbrückengasse subway station. They had gone into the most elegant boutiques on Kärntnerstrasse and on the Graben and Madalyn had tried on outrageously expensive clothes and Moritz had pretended to have a Russian accent and be the son of an oligarch or somebody like that. Madalyn had rehearsed with him beforehand and even downloaded some Russian words from the internet and written them down on a piece of paper. They also visited furniture stores (Frau Moser's store for example, which was right on their way home from school, less than two hundred yards from the Rahlgasse). He had told Madalyn she ought to be an actress, really. She had natural talent. As soon as she was discovered he bet she would be in the movies in a flash and make piles of money. – I wanted to interrupt him and ask, *She* would make money? Only her? Why are you using the singular? Don't you picture yourself at her side? Not even in pretend? Listen, I wanted to say to him, don't you feel the magic she spreads over everything? Over the deadly boring boutiques in the deadly boring center of town, over our tame Danube, over the cities of Chicago, New York, and Paris, and over the great continent of Africa? Haven't you seen it, heard it, felt it, I wanted to ask him. Don't you know that a person in love can found a new world? That's what I would have liked to ask.

 When he learned that Madalyn was really supposed to move to a foreign city with her parents, far away from Vienna, he realized that it was not a game for Madalyn and probably never had been. She told Moritz that the time had come. He had promised her, and now their time had come. She wanted to run away right now. With him. He had to keep his word. And he had beaten around the bush and said it was too early and stuff like that. It was true that he'd promised her, but he thought the promise was just pretend too. Finally he had to admit that he didn't want to leave. At least, not yet. He definitely wanted to finish school first. Then he would take off with her. Cross his heart. She had said, If I have to go to Hong Kong we'll never see each other again. Never again. She knew for certain he wouldn't wait two years for her. He said he would, absolutely, cross his heart. But it didn't help. She said she wouldn't be able to stand it in Hong Kong. She didn't know anybody there and she didn't want to know anybody. And the whole time she would be alone with her mother. And she cried. He couldn't get her to calm down.

And now he was crying too.

"But," he said, "I can't just go away. And we just don't have enough money. She hasn't thought it through."

"And now she's taken off on her own? Is that what you think, Moritz?"

"I don't know. I really don't know."

"And you have no idea where she is?"

He covered his face with his hands and gave a little scream.

"Please Moritz," I said and took him by the upper arms. "Please tell me everything you know!"

"I don't know where she is. Honest I don't. I just don't know. She's so unpredictable."

"What do you mean, unpredictable?"

"She might flip out."

"Is she in the house by the Old Danube? Is she there? Tell me, is she there?"

He looked at me and just shrugged his shoulders. And I got really frighteneed.

"You think she's there, don't you? Why didn't you go there? Did you ride over there? Talk to me! Why didn't you ride over there, Moritz! Why didn't you go see!"

He tipped over sideways, lay on the bench, buried his face in his arms and cried and thrashed his legs like an angry child.

Chapter Twenty-Eight

I ran out of the park into the Wienzeile and headed toward Kettenbrückengasse. As I ran I reached into my pocket to make sure I had enough money and hailed a cab at the end of the Naschmarkt. It was midday traffic. I asked the driver to hurry and offered him double the amount to drive fast. I said it was my daughter and I hoped she was all right. He stepped on the gas, squeezed past the waiting line of cars, honked, drove onto the sidewalk, all the while not saying a word and avoiding looking at me in the rearview mirror. We were able go faster through the second district. I got out at the bridge near the Old Danube subway station. He wouldn't take any money, drove off without saying goodbye.

From what Madalyn had told me, I could estimate how long it would take to get to the house on foot. I hoped I would recognize it. I ran down the steps to the water. A bicycle was leaning against the trash containers at the beginning of the row of weekend houses. I jumped onto it and rode as fast as I could past the first houses.

She had described the house very precisely, the tall conifer in front, the palm tree, the broken statue, and the turquoise façade. I jumped off the bike and scrambled over the fence. It was in fact no great feat to open the back door. I called her name, ran upstairs, tore open the doors. The house was empty. Dusty, filthy, musty, dark, and empty.

I sat down on the stairs and didn't know what to do. There were still remnants of the candles there, a circle of candles in the midst of which Moritz and Madalyn had sat. When had that been? Two months ago? If Madalyn's story was right.

"Please, Madalyn," I said, "please, please, don't do this to me!"

There were cigarette butts lying around, some only half smoked. I found a box of matches underneath the stairs. I lit up one of the butts. My first lungful for two years. And when I finished that one, I lit another.

Of course I thought about my father, which I hadn't done in a long time. But I didn't think about him with pain and a bad conscience as I had for so many years. I was frightened by my voice in this strange house. As if I was planning on using the situation for a movie. After they told me on the telephone that he had taken his own life – that was thirty-three years ago; I was twenty-six – I had marched briskly through Frankfurt, talking to the pavement beneath my feet, a word at each step, every step a word. Why. Are. You. Doing. This. To. Me. I left my light on at night. I didn't want to hide. I felt like a bad person because I could only think that it was like a movie and could only act like I was in a movie. My apartment on Danneckerstrasse seemed like a movie set. And what really felt like a movie was that I didn't want to feel like I was in a movie. Robert had once told me that I divided humanity into two categories: into potential suicides and not potential suicides. Everybody else was in the first category and only I was in the second. Which made me universally susceptible to blackmail.

The floor was covered with footprints in the dust and sand, with rat droppings, extinguished matches, squashed cigarette butts, and bottle caps. And yet – and although the windows were boarded shut and the drapes moldering and only a thin light filtered through – there were benevolent spirits in this room, spirits that resisted being represented on the screen.

As I came out of the house I discovered a man standing in front of me. He was shorter than me, but a good half belt wider. He wore an old brown lumberjack coat that was too small for him. He wanted to know what I was doing here. Who the hell was I, anyway? He told me not to move.

"I can explain it to you," I said. "This house belongs to the boyfriend of the aunt of a friend of mine. It's true. I was just looking to see if he was here."

"That's bullshit," he said. "This house belongs to me. What's all this crap you're talking about!"

"Then you must know Moritz Kaltenegger," I said. "You must be his aunt's boyfriend."

"You're full of shit," he screamed. He said he was going to call the police. He'd finally caught the asshole who'd been breaking into his house. He put his arm across my throat and pressed me against the wall while he pulled his cell phone out of his pocket. The only thing I could do was to scream at him in my turn. I yelled as loud as I could, pushed him off, and ran around the house. I heard him coming after me but I didn't turn around. I got over the fence, left the bicycle where it was, and took off running while thinking that he would grab the bike and catch up with me. If he runs he won't catch me. He's too fat. But he'll come after me on the bike and then he'll knock me over and break my neck. And I could feel my thighs getting soft and wobbly because I was running out of steam.

He wasn't running or riding after me. He was protecting his property.

So the little rat had been lying again, I thought. He can't stop lying, he can't help himself. His aunt probably didn't even have a boyfriend. Maybe he didn't even have an aunt. I stopped in the middle of the bridge, spread my arms wide on the railing, bent over, and struggled for breath.

I didn't know if giving Madalyn the key to my apartment was technically procuring. It didn't take a lot of imagination to picture what kind of ruckus Frau Reis would raise if she found out about it. But it surely would have taken a great deal of imagination to explain to her what had moved me to do it. I was a fool -- I was only half a fool; it was clear to me that now I had to deliver the other half.

Later, Frau Moser told me about how the two of them had visited her store. At first she thought they were just play-acting, having her on. "The girl said she was from Germany. She was a violinist studying at the conservatory in Vienna. The young man was a cellist. They had rented a studio together. They pretended they were musical prodigies everyone had heard of and were looking for some furniture for their studio. They only wanted to see the most beautiful things because it was impossible to make beautiful music in ugly surroundings, the girl said. He didn't say much." Frau Moser ended up believing every word they said. She asked Madalyn if she and her friends were going to perform some time in Vienna. And Madalyn had named a date and place without a moment's hesitation.

But even had Frau Moser told me about this incident earlier, it wouldn't have made much difference. Someone invents their own reality – is the necessary consequence that you don't need to take them seriously in their desperation? It was completely understandable that Moritz wanted nothing to do with the police. Unfortunately, I was not going to be able to spare him that.

And I was not going to be able to spare myself the trouble of having to ring the bell of the apartment directly below mine after all.

Chapter Twenty-Nine

Herr Reis opened the door. He asked at once if I was there because of Madalyn. He looked exhausted, considerably older than I remembered him, less attractive. His hair was lighter. Not gray, just lighter. I didn't recognize him immediately.

"Yes," I said.

"How so?" he asked, widening his eyes.

"I've talked to Madalyn's boyfriend."

"Madalyn's boyfriend? She has a boyfriend? How do you know? I didn't know that. How come *you* know about it?"

"He told me." It wasn't a lie, at least not directly. Moritz probably would have told me if I had acted like I didn't know who he was. I couldn't explain to Madalyn's father why his daughter had told the story of her love to *me* and not to *him*. I couldn't explain it to myself, either.

"And why did he tell you and not me or my wife?"

"I don't know." Should I have said, Because he guessed that Madalyn was at my place?

"Is he in Madalyn's school? Why didn't he talk to the police? The police were at the school." Should I have said, Because he's already been caught breaking into a cigarette machine and has a record? If that's the way to say it in the case of a minor.

He asked me to come in. His wife wasn't at home, he said. She was talking to one of Madalyn's girlfriends. Madalyn has no girlfriends, I could have told him. I could also have asked him if he had any idea why his daughter hadn't come home. If he could imagine that she was unhappy with something at home. He led me into the kitchen. The cupboards were closed, the dishwasher was empty and shiny clean, and it smelled like nothing. In the middle of the table was a glass of water – like in the room of Lodovico Settembrini in *The Magic Mountain*. It could just as well have been a vase of flowers as a drinking glass. Herr Reis was in his stocking feet. He asked if he could offer me something. "A glass of water for me too," I said. He drew it from the tap while holding his Blackberry in one hand. An unwrapped bar of chocolate lay on the dishwasher. I asked if I could have a piece. My blood sugar level was way down.

I told him what Moritz had told me. That he and Madalyn had been pretending they were going to run away. I said nothing about Africa or Chicago or New York, nor about Russian oligarchs or stock market speculations or beggar women experiencing a miracle.

"The best thing would be for me to go right to the police," I said, "and tell it to them. I just wanted to talk to you and your wife beforehand."

He thanked me, but his eyes told me that he didn't know what he was thanking me for. "And there's nothing you know that you don't want to tell me?"

I made sure to sound hostile: "Such as?"

"Can't you imagine how desperate my wife and I are?"

I would have loved to worm my way out of this movie and not just out of this scene – out of the entire movie. I was a better actor than he was, although he wasn't acting and I was. I knew myself. I wasn't as heartless as I felt.

I met Frau Reis at the police station on Schönbrunnerstrasse. Her husband had called her up. She had driven right over in a taxi. She was waiting for me at the front entrance. She looked calm, alert, and energetic, as if she was expecting only the best. She put her hands on my shoulder blades and hugged me to her. She said her husband had told her everything. He was going to stay at home in case Madalyn might show up there (i.e., sneak into the apartment, pack a few clothes, and then disappear, never to be seen again, I thought).

I gave my name, profession, address, and telephone number and told the two officers – a man and a woman – my half-truths, gave Moritz Kaltenegger's full name, and said he was one class above Madalyn.

The policeman asked me how I knew all that. He sat with half his backside on the edge of the formica table, scratched his knee with his thumb, and didn't seem uneasy but not uninterested either. I replied that Madalyn had told me about it. Unlike her husband, Frau Reis didn't ask me why her daughter had talked to me and not to her. She nodded, smiled, and looked steadily at me as I spoke. As if she was proud of me. As if she and I had discussed what I would say.

I don't know what set off the next thing that happened. The policewoman had obviously insinuated something and Frau Reis flew off the handle. Without any warning. She screamed so loudly that the woman took a step backwards and clasped her hands behind her back. I concluded that she must have insinuated something from the tirade that now broke over us.

"This man," shouted Frau Reis in a tone of voice that was curiously familiar to me, as if I had been expecting it, "this man here saved my daughter's life when she was five years old. Have you ever saved anyone's life? Or is taking a life all you know how to do? This man and my daughter have had a special relationship ever since. You don't have to drag it through the mud. I won't allow anyone to do that, you hear me? He's her guardian angel. Of course you don't have enough imagination and sympathy in your tiny brain to understand that. You sit around here on your fat bottom with your belt all loaded down with a cell phone, a nightstick, a gun, and a Leatherman, not lifting a finger to find my daughter but insulting the best friend she has in the world. Do you even know who this man is? Of course you don't! He's one of the most important authors in our country . . ." And so on. Frau Reis was my defense attorney. She was praising me to the skies just as, on another occasion, she had condemned someone else – her daughter, for example – to hell and would do so again. She apologized to me for the behavior of the police. Apologized for the shape our republic was in, where the justice minister protected a notorious lawbreaker and a fourteen-year-old burglar could be shot in the back by the police and nothing would be done about it.

The policewoman listened to all this as if she was one of many students in a training course, probably one of the slower ones. When the outburst was over she took my personal information and without seeming in the least perturbed, said I should remain available and if possible not turn off my cell phone, at least not in the next forty-eight hours.

"Aren't you going to apologize to this man?" hissed Frau Reis.

The policewoman didn't answer. During Frau Reis's tirade, the policeman had just held up his hands in an attempt to placate her but had said nothing.

Outside, Frau Reis asked if it was all right with me if we walked home together. She needed some fresh air. Her anger was extinguished. She didn't say a single word about it. Fortunately, it wasn't more than a ten-minute walk.

She wasn't worried. She said she was, but she wasn't. She told me that when she was a girl, she had run away from home three or four times. Not because she had anything against her parents, who had been fine people. She simply couldn't help herself. As a child, she sometimes got the urge to throw herself on the ground and embrace the world, or punch it. She had grown up in the country, where there was plenty of world to be hugged or punched. – Meanwhile, I was completely silent. Not intentionally. Because I wanted to see if she would notice at some point. She didn't.

When we reached her apartment door, she asked if I'd like to come in. She said she had a terribly bad conscience about me. Because of back then. Because she simply left me standing there in the hospital. She had always wanted to apologize and to thank me, but she was afraid I would reject her. Until at last, it was simply too late. She had talked to Madalyn about me many times. Madalyn had said I certainly wasn't mad at her. I was a very distinguished person. She kept planning to invite me to dinner. But first of all, she wasn't a good cook – Madalyn was much better – and second, she was too embarrassed.

"It's all right," I said. "I hope Madalyn will get in touch soon."

Then she said to me, "Don't worry about it."

I guessed that she knew what was up with Madalyn. I guessed that the two of them were allies against the man who wanted to drag them off to Hong Kong. For the sake of his career.

I went up to my apartment with the sobering feeling that I was now clear of it all.

Chapter Thirty

Madalyn had in fact called her mother. She said she felt like her mother had felt when she ran away from home three or four times as a child. She too had suddenly felt the urge to hug the world or punch in. She said she was with a girlfriend but wouldn't tell who it was. She would come home tomorrow. – How do I know all this? Madalyn told me herself.

When I got home, she was curled up asleep on the green leather chair in the library. I said her name and she woke up.

She was greatly changed. Pale, her eyes bleary and puffy. Her hair had gotten longer again; her curls were disheveled. Her face had a bewildered earnestness. I said she couldn't stay here. I had just been at the police station with her mother. She had to go downstairs immediately. Immediately. I wasn't angry, but I tried to seem angry.

"Leave, please!" I commanded and then told another lie. "Your mother is crazy with worry."

That's when she told me she had phoned her mother that afternoon.

"What about your father?"

"Maybe she's already told him, maybe not. Depends on his mood. Before they go to bed, she'll tell him. She'll pretend I just called up and then she'll tell him."

"That's crazy," I said.

"She doesn't want to spoil my game," she replied.

I was so confused that the obvious question only now occurred to me. How did she get into my apartment, anyway, huh? She got in with my extra key. On Easter Sunday she'd simply left a different key on the kitchen table. That had been her very own idea. She figured I would put it back where I kept it without trying it out. All house keys look alike anyway. She left me her own key to their apartment instead and told her parents she had lost it. Her mother had made a scene and gotten a new one made for her. And if I had noticed, she would simply have said it was a mistake. That was all.

"Why did you do that, Madalyn?"

She just looked at me and nodded.

"Were you two here often?"

"I told you you wouldn't notice anything."

What a solitary person I've become! I get up at precisely the same time every morning, go have breakfast in the coffee house at precisely the same time, sit down at my computer at precisely the same time, make myself a little something to eat while I listen to the news on the radio at precisely the same time. And every afternoon I take the U4 and the U1 to the Prater, walk the main promenade from one end to the other and back, then ride into town, shop for a few things I need, browse the bookstores and CD shops or meet Robert Lenobel or Hanna or whoever, and after four hours, I'm back home. A calculable, solitary man.

"That really hurts me," I said. "Do you realize that?"

She twitched her shoulders and so much misery rose into her eyes.

"I'm very angry," I said. But I wanted to hug her and say it's going to be all right.

Because nothing was all right.

Chapter Thirty-One

Nothing was all right.

Oh, that stuff with China, it wasn't that! She didn't even think about that anymore. For her mother it was a horrible thought. Madalyn didn't care by now. Once when they were in my apartment he had fallen asleep but she couldn't sleep. His rucksack was out in the hall and she had heard his cell phone signal an incoming text message. And then another. She got up and went out, knelt beside his rucksack and waited for another signal. And suddenly, she didn't know why, she had taken his phone out of the side pocket and looked at the text message. It was from Claudia. She had written that she loved him. And the second message was from her too. It said that she gotten her period. Which Madalyn didn't get right away. Then she got it, but when she went back into the room and saw him lying there with one hand over his eyes because the sun was shining in the window onto his face, she didn't get it again and went back into the hall and looked at the two messages again. She sat down on the toilet and waited. Sometimes it could happen that a text message got lost and only popped up a long time later. It had never happened to her, but it could happen. She wanted it so much to be a technical error. And she went over to his rucksack again, looked to see when the messages had been sent, and saw that it was not a technical error. She went back into the room and lay down next to him. He woke up and embraced her and she embraced him. He looked at the clock and jumped up because their time had run out. He arranged everything the way it had been and she helped. They had agreed that he would always take the elevator down while she walked down the stairs and that he would wait for out on the Wienzeile. Today she wanted to take the elevator down with him. She was afraid to walk down four flights of stairs alone. Afraid of all that would be racing through her head and afraid of who she would be when she reached the bottom. While they were in the elevator, his cell phone beeped again. He pretended it was nothing. He didn't flinch or look funny. Afterwards, she had sometimes walked part way with him or they had strolled around in the fourth district together. But usually, they parted at the Naschmarkt. That's what she preferred, because after their two or three hours she liked to put her head back together piece by piece. In just one month she had become a good student. She had taken three tests, in English, German, and French, and got a good grade in all three subjects and just barely missed getting an A in English, and only got a B in German on account of all the spelling and punctuation errors, but as far as content was concerned, it had been the best test in the class. Plus two quizzes in geography and history. And she hadn't even studied very hard – it had seemed to come automatically. She heard something and remembered it. Never in her life had she been so happy to be alone. And now she didn't know how she was going to go on. If he turned around and left, she didn't know what would happen inside of her. He would leave and as soon as she couldn't see him anymore, he'd look at his cell phone. And return the messages. She said she'd like to walk him home today. In the subway she sat next to him so she wouldn't have to look into his face. She stared straight ahead. But he didn't see it. He asked her why she wasn't talking. She had no idea what she ought to say. On Stuwerstrasse she asked him if she could come up with him. She had never been to his house. He said she was welcome to if she wanted, but things hadn't been straightened up, a horrible pigsty, and his aunt was probably in a bad mood because it was his turn to clean up and he hadn't done it. She could help him clean, she said. In the subway, he'd gotten another text message. He had reached into his rucksack, glanced quickly at it, and turned off the phone. Again, without looking any special way. It could be, she thought, that Claudia just tried to reach him again and again and he just didn't react, just looked at the screen, didn't answer, and turned it off. She knew he had slept with her. And if Claudia had just pretended that her period was late, Madalyn had heard things like that before. But she didn't believe it. She really did want to help him clean up his room. It would have been so intimate. She liked to straighten up at home. She listened to music while she did it and followed a precise plan. She was welcome to come up, he repeated. He had told his aunt a lot about her, and her aunt's boyfriend too. His eyelids were drooping as if he had drunk something. It was the way he looked when he had had a couple beers. But he hadn't drunk anything. She was frightened because she had to think, he'll take me up with him, but just before he opens the door, some reason will occur to him why it would be better if I didn't go in. And she didn't want to risk that, so she said she'd better be going home after all. He spoke quite calmly. The way he did when he'd had a couple beers. She was welcome to come up, he repeated. She could have supper with them and watch some TV afterwards. His aunt would be happy to meet her and so would her boyfriend. She left without giving him a kiss.

She slept deeply that night and woke up in the morning feeling like a murderer after the deed. That had always seemed like the worst thing to her. She realized with horror that Moritz must have seen that someone had accessed the two text messages. Who else but her, of course! She would just deny everything. She couldn't get any breakfast down, and went to school. If a classmate had not given her a bar of chocolate, she would have been nauseous. She usually hung out with him near the Rahlstiege in the long recess. She'd take a drag of his cigarette but didn't inhale. She liked the smell of cigarettes but not the taste. Sometimes he wasn't in the schoolyard during recess. Then he would text her to say he was doing homework for the following day or had to learn something fast for a test in the next period – stuff like that. Since she had gotten to be such a good student he wanted to be a good student too. He often said that to her. He said, You're making me a better person. She liked hearing that. It's the most beautiful thing you can say to someone. She tried to recall the past days. Had there been anything else? She couldn't think of anything. When would he have gotten together with Claudia? When could it have been? She thought it could only have been in the evening. She was allowed to go out on weekends but not on weekdays. But, she thought, Claudia must know that I'm his girlfriend. Everybody knows it. Even his friends at the Flex know it. She wouldn't want him to have two girlfriends, her and another girl, would she? No one wants that. And what does he tell her? When had she seen Claudia last? She kept her ears open and found out that Claudia wasn't even in school anymore. She'd just stopped coming, in the middle of the year. No one knew why.

Soon they weren't meeting so often anymore. She definitely didn't want it to get to be an annoying routine. He said he was stressed out in school. In two subjects he was fairly weak and he needed to study. Instead, he texted her more often. When they were together, she felt like it was even better than it had been. They were phoning each other just as much. In that regard, there wasn't any suspicious change.

But then she saw him in a bus and the girl was clearly Claudia and they were clearly kissing. And it was a real kiss, that was clear too. And what's more, Moritz saw her standing outside the bus. He saw her and didn't stop kissing. She had to sit down on the wall beside the Haus des Meeres aquarium and she was crying so hard that one of the homeless guys sitting there with their dogs and their bottles of beer came over with his dog and his bottle and sat down next to her without saying anything, and his dog lay down in front of her so its side was against her leg. That's exactly what it did, she said. She couldn't see very well through all the tears, but her cell phone signaled that a text message had come: "Now you know, but you don't know anything."

She didn't want to know anything, either.

He had an explanation. After he'd told Claudia they were through and he had a new girlfriend, she had broken down. She lay in bed at home and cried for days. He had felt like a killer. She stopped going to school. Her parents called in a doctor who urged them to start her in therapy. She'd slit her wrist. She wanted to die. That's what she wrote him and he rushed over to see her. She was at home alone and he had pounded on the door until she let him in. She had wrapped a bandage around her wrist and it was bloody. He had taken a look at the wound and helped her to bandage it better. And she had said she would do it again. If he left her she would do it again. He had been desperate and finally said he would come back to her. But he hadn't slept with her. And he hadn't really gone back to her, either, not in his heart. He just said that to calm her down. He just talked to her and sometimes he kissed her because he was afraid that if he didn't, it would start all over again. At some point she claimed she was pregnant – just claimed to be. A lie; she was desperate. He was at his wits' end, didn't know what to do. When Madalyn saw him and Claudia in the bus, things had been especially critical. He thought it would get better with time. He wanted to take it slowly, let it fade out, slowly. The best thing would be to make himself boring. That was his plan.

That's what he'd told Madalyn yesterday. She hadn't seen him or phoned him since then. He'd tried calling her almost a hundred times and sent her twenty texts.

Chapter Thirty-Two

I said, "do you believe him, Madalyn?"
She nodded vigorously.
I said, "He's lying." I paced up and down in front of her while I lectured. "He's a liar. It's all lies."

I saw him again in my mind's eye, the way he tipped over on the bench and shook with the strength of his crying and thrashed his legs at me. And suddenly, while I was still trying to convince Madalyn, I thought, No, it's all true. He's not lying. Everybody thinks he's a liar, but he's not. Would a liar admit that he had plagiarized a poem? Everybody thought he had written it, even the teacher who knew so much about literature, and he admits it to the very person he most wants to impress? Without being forced to and not at some random time, but the first time they were together. He looks at you out of the corner of his eye and if you look back, he can grin as if to say, you know what's up, but don't tell anyone else. He makes himself into an accomplice of his own bad reputation. At some point, the false liar became inscribed on his face. And now everyone can see it and everyone thinks they have the proof. But are they wrong? *Now you know, but you don't know anything.* And that horrific story about his mother and her lover that he laid out for Madalyn on the telephone – I didn't believe it for a second. But why would he have told it to her if it wasn't true? What did he have to gain? A psychological explanation for his constant mendacity, and thus a pardon for his lies and a license to keep on lying? Is that how a sixteen-year-old thinks? It's how a sixty-year-old thinks. As if I were looking into a mirror that made the image into its negative. I never had any trouble lying to someone. I'm the guy everyone believes even if he's lying. By the way, I consider this talent as a kind of psychological collateral damage from my profession. He speaks the truth and is more lonely than any liar. And Madalyn is the only one who believes him.

"Where were you last night?" I asked

"Out walking in the city."

"And where did you sleep?"

"I didn't sleep."

"You didn't sleep at all?"

"Nope, not at all."

"And you just walked around?"

"At first I sat on a bench by the Danube Canal. But then I thought, Man, he might come by here, like if he was at the Flex or something. That wouldn't be good, and I was afraid too, because it was so dark, and I was shivering in the cold coming up from the water."

"And you really weren't at anybody's house?"

"No. I told you."

"And what did you do after you left the Danube Canal?"

"Walked into town."

"What time was that?"

"About one, I guess. There were still a lot of people on the street."

"Nobody walks around in town all night long. I don't believe you."

"I didn't walk around all night."

"So what *did* you do?"

"I sat down somewhere."

"Where?"

"Just somewhere."

"Don't you want to tell me?"

"In front of the Burgtheater."

"I beg your pardon?"

"At the Burgtheater, on the steps that go up to the front entrance. It was only 2:30. I saw it on the town hall clock. Because I was afraid to go into the Rathaus Park or any other park, but I was already really tired. And from the steps I had a good view of everything. There are a couple of doors and I sat in front of the one on the far left. You can't always be seen there right away. But I didn't sleep. I stroked my hair. That's what I did. The whole time. And then it got to be too cold, and I started walking around again."

The doorbell rang.

Madalyn's father stood at the door. A man with a big smile on his face. He rested his hands on the door frame and one leg was crossed over the other. He just wanted to let me know that Madalyn had called up his wife, thank God. She said she was at a girlfriend's house and would come home tomorrow, thank God.

"Thank God," I agreed.

When I got back to the library, Madalyn was gone.

Chapter Thirty-Three

She was standing on the roof terrace outside my study, on the outside of the railing. Her back was turned to me. She had hooked her arms over the railing behind her and was looking down into the interior courtyard. I wasn't sure she knew I was there. But I knew what she was intending to do.

And so I told her about my father. She tilted her head toward me a little. I spoke softly, on purpose. And I told her why. "I don't want anyone else to hear me. See, no one needs to find out about my father. It's no one else's business. And I'm very angry at you because I have to tell you this story." She didn't respond. And she didn't turn around to me. The right thing would probably have been for me to creep up and grab hold of her from behind. But what if I couldn't hang onto her? She was standing on the outer edge of the lead flashing that jutted out a little beyond the terrace edge and I didn't know how stabile it was. Besides, it had been drizzling that afternoon and the metal was slippery. I didn't want to have to be a hero even if I could. I told her about my father. I've done it a few times before when I had to soften someone up. It's certainly underhanded to use the death of a relative to talk someone out of something. I've had recourse to this scam on much less serious occasions, and it worked. He was alone when he did it. It was my mother who found him. He was lying on his mattress with a wool blanket pulled over his head and his feet sticking out the other end. He was barefoot. Even if someone sees through your deceit, it still has a satisfying effect. Because no one dares not to pay obeisance to the dead, or to their survivors either. My mother was bringing him something to eat. By that time he was hardly eating anything. Nor did he need much whiskey anymore. He had swallowed pills. I told Madalyn that I took off for America after his death. And finally I said, "Madalyn, don't do this to me.

The police are going to question me. Did you think of that? Don't you care? They're going to find out that you've been in my apartment with Moritz. They're going to find out that I gave you my key. You're under age. I've probably broken the law. Did you know that? They won't believe me that you switched the keys. They'll think I let you use the apartment for all this time. They'll put me in jail. They'll put me in jail for criminal negligence and involuntary manslaughter. Why don't you care about me? I cared about you. You said yourself that I had made everything turn out all right. Why are you making everything bad for me now?" – I was ashamed of myself. Ashamed of my whining tone. If this ends well, I thought, I'll never be able to look her in the eye again. Neither of us will ever be able to look the other in the eye again. – "Why did you pick me of all people to do this shit to?" I growled at her. "I saved your life when you were five and now you're wrecking mine. It's not fair."

"Why did your father do it?" she asked softly.

You could have seen her from the balcony of the floor below. Her parents were non-smokers. It would have been a typical smokers' balcony, an ashtray full of butts and matchboxes full of used matches. And who will move in when they're gone? People who'll want to crane their necks to look up and chat with me? And what will happen to the table with the head of Botticelli's Venus? I could act like I'd gone crazy. Somebody told me once about how four guys had wanted to beat him up in the subway one night. They'd jostled him and pushed him around from one to the other. In his fear he had played the halfwit: he babbled the Lord's Prayer hysterically, sang the Horst Wessel song, and pretended to be Hitler making a garbled speech at a Nuremberg rally and giving the Nazi salute. He'd scratched his head like a madman and waved his hands in the air. They either got spooked or figured it wasn't worth beating up a nut job and they left him in peace.

"Why did he do it?" she asked again.

"Because he would have drunk himself to death otherwise, that's why."

"I see."

"He was fifty-four years old. I've already outlived him by five years."

If I was in her place, I thought, and somebody tried out their sentimental stuff on me, I'd jump just because I'd feel ashamed for humanity in general. Which would be a good idea in any case. You stupid idiot, humanity! Should I tell her that? Maybe I could get her to laugh.

I was at my wits' end.

"Please, Madalyn," I said, "please come to me."

And she climbed over the railing and came to me. I put my arm around her and asked if she'd like to have a cup of cocoa with me. She said she'd like that. We descended the spiral staircase and sat down in the kitchen.

"I like the way you have your hair now, very much," I said. "Looks really good on you."

"Really?" she asked.

"Very much. I like your hair and that yellow thistle-cap too, sitting in the moon on the green spider and thinking about street names as if cinnamon stars and white ravens and pealing bells grew out of them . . ." – and Madalyn continued in the same tone as if it were the most natural thing in the world – "because it's well known that if you can talk them into it, the pears in the garden will turn into apples and the apples into chimney- sweeps and the chimney-sweeps into squids that you put into the dryer overnight and by the next morning they've gobbled up so much sauerkraut that they . . . that they . . . that they . . . I can't think of what comes next. Please, tell him," she begged me softly. "Tell him I was going to jump. And that you saved my life again. You could wait for him after school. He always rides the same way. Out the Gumpendorferstrasse and across Schillerplatz to the Ring and along the Ring as far as the Urania and across the bridge. Please tell him. Promise?"

"I promise."

I called up Evelyn and she was there in fifteen minutes. She took Madalyn home with her and made up a bed on the sofa. But Evelyn said that in the night, Madalyn came and asked if she could crawl in bed with her.

Chapter Thirty-Four

I couldn't stand to remain in Vienna. I was having a quiet period and was able to concentrate on my work (which meant that my hero was managing to free himself from his real-life model). But I wasn't satisfied. Everything that seemed beautiful to me about the spring was a memory of former springs. That's not the way to approach the seasons. I visited Hanna and Robert more often than before and frequently stayed the night at Evelyn's. One weekend we went to Budapest together. From the restaurant of our hotel we watched two men in the street arguing over a woman, not angrily but very intensely. At least, that's how we interpreted the scene. In the train on the way back, Evelyn curled up on the seat and put her head in my lap.

On short notice, I booked a flight to Lisbon. As a child, I'd lived there for half a year. I went walking through Alfama and sat down under a tree in front of a tiny café with my notebook. And thought about nothing.

In June the Reis family moved to Hong Kong. A few days before they left, Madalyn showed up at my door to say that her parents wanted to invite me to dinner. I was the only person in the whole building they had a relationship with. With her hands she put quotation marks around the word "relationship" and winked at me. I was welcome to bring a guest along. She, Madalyn, would really like it if Evelyn came too. And then she got very serious and I knew that I would miss that serious face. We both were unsure of ourselves and finding this difficult. But in a bit we were able to look each other in the eye. She started, and I was able to withstand her gaze. It was hard for me. I didn't want to invite her in. I said I would prefer it if she didn't expect me to invite her in. She rolled her eyes and smiled and her lips silently repeated my contorted sentence. She said she'd like to come in anyway.

The way she walked through the apartment, I could tell she would rather have been alone. I asked if she wanted to be alone and she nodded. I left.

I called up Evelyn on my cell phone. "I'll pick you up from the museum," I said.

I waited by the fountain in front of the Karlskirche and watched the seagulls.

"You and I are invited to dinner," I said and told her that Madalyn was saying goodbye to my apartment.

Evelyn said nothing to that. She only said she didn't want to. Didn't want to go to Madalyn's parents' place. Absolutely not.

And so I went down by myself that evening. There were three different salads as hors-d'oeuvres, prepared by Madalyn. They were delicious. I happened to bring three things for dessert, too: dark chocolate mousse, white chocolate mousse, and lemon mint mousse. I got them from Cantinetta Antinori. They usually don't do take-out, but for me they made an exception.

CPSIA information can be obtained
at www.ICGtesting.com
Printed in the USA
FSOW02n0624130516
20303FS

9 781572 412002